The Horsemaster's Daughter

by

Grace Colline

The Horsemaster's Daughter

Cover Art by *The Wild Rose Press, Inc.*

The Wild Rose Press, Inc.
PO Box 708
Adams Basin, NY 14410-0708
Visit us at www.thewildrosepress.com

Publishing History
First Edition, 2024
Trade Paperback ISBN 978-1-5092-5773-7
Digital ISBN 978-1-5092-5774-4

Published in the United States of America

Other Books By Grace Colline

The Lady and the Lieutenant

Chapter One

Cold, drizzly rain met William as he stepped out of the carriage. He ducked under the umbrella offered by the footman and trudged up to the manor. Underneath the archway, into the courtyard, up the steps to where the dowager duchess stood waiting.

"Good. You're here. Finally."

"Carriage only goes so fast, Mother."

"I expected you last night."

"Had to feed and rest the horses." He shed his overcoat and gloves, handing them to a waiting servant and followed his mother up the staircase.

"The funeral is in three days' time."

"That soon?"

"There is no need to wait."

They turned a corner and entered the large double doors into his father's bedchamber. Tapestries lined the walls, but the fireplace was cold, and he turned to the figure on the bed. Lined face smoothed in death, the tenth Duke of Tensington lay still upon the crimson coverlet. Dressed in his black suit he looked even more forbidding than he had in life. The eleventh duke stared down at his father, willing some faint vestige of grief to well up within.

There was none.

His father had been a distant, cold, man who had cared more for his horses than for his son. To them he had given love and patience, acceptance and time. To his son, only stern distance spawned of disappointment.

His mother's voice broke into his thoughts. "What are your plans?"

William looked down at her from his height and shook his head. "I don't know what you mean. I have my own estate to run."

"It is Withcombe that matters. You must come home."

"This isn't my home. Besides, where would I stay?"

"Here, in the duke's chamber."

"Where my father died?"

"And his father before him. Likely most of the Dukes of Tensington."

William grimaced and looked away. He thought of Marwinne, his own little estate nearly fifty miles hence near the town of Sattersby. A bit small—traditionally it was the dower house—and yet it felt more like home than the rambling halls and painted rooms of Withcombe. But now, his father lay dead and his mother would be expecting to move into his home while he came here. The thought nearly brought him to tears.

He hated Withcombe, its pretentiousness, its traditions, and most of all—its stables. For it was in the stables that Withcombe's prizes dwelled. Horses.

For over a century, Withcombe had been famous for its horses. The "Withcombe Bay," bred from a line of Cleveland Bays and Thoroughbreds, was highly sought after by sportsmen even beyond Britain's shores.

Horses.

He shrugged off the thought. Glancing over at his

mother, he noted again how she had aged, withered even. He could not burden her with the estate, but neither would he banish her from her home. It would be her choice where she wanted to live, here, or the dower house. He sighed and turned away.

"What do you need me to do, Mother?"

"You can check on the infernal horses for one. I've spoken to the housekeeper and the butler about the funeral. Your father wished to be interred in the chapel and had selected a space which is being prepared. I have everything well in hand, but the stables have been neglected. I fear that Basque Mondragón has had free rein for far too long."

"I'll go check on the stables. Anything I should know?"

"Do not ask me. Your father did not divulge his precious plans to me."

"Right." He kissed his mother's cheek, grinning at the shocked expression on her face, and headed off toward the prize of Withcombe—its stables.

They comprised several buildings, including a set of pastures where mares heavy with foal grazed, the stables proper, a training course and ring, and the horsemaster's home—a compact, two-story cottage with a narrow stoop. As he passed the ring, a fine young stallion was being trained by one of the younger boys. He wondered vaguely where old Arnas was. The horsemaster usually did not let others handle his training.

He headed directly for the door and rang the bell, hearing it echo from deep within. A bark, followed by another answered the bell. Then, a thump and slide sound grew louder as it came closer, and the door was flung open by a powerfully built man leaning on a cane.

"Who is it…oh, your grace. My apologies." Arnas Mondragón stood bent, leaning on his cane, dark hair turned gray at the temples.

William had always been afraid of him. Now he towered over the horsemaster. An old dog hovered at Arnas' knees and William fought to remember its name.

"Zigor, back," Arnas said and the mystery was solved.

William smiled briefly. "I passed by a fine-looking stallion out in the ring. Which one is it?"

Arnas looked out from under his beret. His expression was somewhat guarded. "That's Hallington's Hope. Our new stallion."

"What happened to old…what's his name?"

"Tunbridge Blue? He's retired."

"What are you going to do with him?"

"Do with him? He will live out his days in peace."

"At my expense, no doubt."

"He's earned it!"

"Well, we shall see. Who was that out in the ring with Hallington's whatever?"

Arnas frowned, "Just some new groom—got a lot of talent. My assistant if you will."

William frowned with the force of remembering. "Didn't you have a daughter, or a granddaughter…used to hang about."

"My daughter, Sarah. She's around."

William nodded and took a deep breath, looking at the buildings which seemed unchanged. His father had dragged him around continuously when he was a child, and he had been happy and willing to be involved in the horses' lives. Until his accident.

He shuddered and pushed the memory aside. He no longer feared the animals, but nor did he love them anymore. He stepped down from Arnas's stoop and strode toward the ring where the slight figure struggled momentarily with the brilliant bay. He watched for a moment, then slid through the railing and proceeded to walk up to them.

The horse turned to look at him, the whites of his eyes showing. He reared up and the groom eased off on the lead, speaking in a soft, low voice. William halted in his progress. Then, when the horse seemed to have calmed, he started forward again.

Hallington's Hope reared again, snatching the lead free from the groom's hands and raced off across the ring. He approached the edge and his hindquarters bunched, then he leapt mightily and cleared the fence. With tail high, he ran off into the trees.

"Damn it!" The groom let out an explosive breath and turned to William. "Who are you to come charging in while I'm training?"

William stared down, for this was no groom before him, but a girl.

Chapter Two

Sarah Mondragón stared up at the stranger, anger roiling through her. Everyone knew to keep their distance with the newest stallion, everyone except this dunderhead, apparently. She looked him up and down, noting the fine clothes and broad shoulders. A deeply buried part of her acknowledged that he was handsome, but at the present moment she was angry and her cheeks burned.

"Who are you?"

He drew himself up and said in a grating voice, "I am William, Duke of Tensington. Who are *you*?"

She turned from him and stomped toward the stables. "Here, Jimmie? Andy? Bring me Cadence and be quick about it." She glanced over at William. "My name is Sarah Mondragón. I'm the horsemaster."

"Arnas Mondragón is the horsemaster. Why are you working with the horses?"

"My father was injured two years ago and forced to retire from active training. He had me take over."

"But you can't...look at you!" He gestured at her loose trousers and knee-high boots.

She shot an incredulous look at him. "Can you see me training horses in all this dirt in a dress and *pelisse*?"

"But it's indecent!"

She reached for a horse led toward her, vaulted

aloft and shook her head as she spurred the horse to action.

Terror erupted through her as she thought about what might happen if Hallington's Hope was injured. All the money sunk into buying him and transporting him to Withcombe could be lost. No, it wasn't her money, but it was the first decision her father had placed on her shoulders. They had travelled about, inspecting horses to replace Blue and found Hope. His name had represented what they needed—hope for the future of Withcombe's stables.

And now the damn horse had raced off into the damn woods and could be anywhere. Behind her the other grooms ran after in pursuit as well, but she knew it was unlikely he would follow any but herself. She had to find him!

She guided Cadence toward the break in the trees where she had seen Hope disappear. Divets of dirt lay scattered by his hooves, and she followed them, thanking the heavens for damp earth. The trail led to a clearing where sun shone down through the open canopy onto a small grassy patch. There stood Hallington's Hope.

His head shot up at her approach, but he didn't shy. With calm, deliberate movements, she dropped down and slowly walked toward the stallion who stood trembling in the midst of the clearing. She noted that he had stepped on his lead, so she reached up to stroke his neck and take control of the taut rope. Then she bent to grasp his fetlock and lift his foot to free the rope.

He resisted at first, but she finally coaxed him to raise his hoof enough to pull the lead loose and grip it tight. Still calmly stroking his neck, she led him back to where Cadence grazed and bent to catch up her reins to lead them both back to the stables. From behind her a horse's hooves sounded and she looked up to see the duke riding rather awkwardly toward her. Blowing out a breath, she stopped the horses and calmed Hope as the duke approached.

He lifted a hand. "I just wanted to apologize for startling the horse. Can I help in any way?"

"Yes, actually. If you would take Cadence and lead her back, I can focus on Hope."

He slowly dropped down. After landing rather heavily on the ground, he grasped his horse's reins. He edged forward to take hold of Cadence and Sarah sighed her relief at being able to focus on Hope.

They walked in silence for some time, Sarah having nothing to say to the new duke. Hope pulled on his lead from time to time, his high-strung antics wearing on Sarah's nerves and arms. Still, she talked calmly to him, stroking the muscled neck from time to time.

Soon they came within sight of the stables and grooms came forward to take the two horses from the duke.

He looked up at Hope. "He seems a fine horse. What's wrong with the old stallion?"

"He's old, in his twenties, unable to perform as well as we need him to. Last year, he was only able to service half the mares."

The duke turned red and his eyebrows shot up. "Does your mother approve of your…interest…with the horses?"

"My mother is dead. My father needs help and mine are the best hands for that. The old duke agreed."

"Father? What?"

"He came by often to talk about the horses with *Aitatxo* and me."

"*Aitatxo?*"

"It is Basque for daddy. It is what I call my father."

"I see."

By this time they had reached the stables. Sarah led the stallion to a stall and called over a groom.

"Get Henry. Tell him I said to rub him down and feed him up."

The lad nodded and rushed off. Sarah's gaze drifted to the duke and she wondered how to politely excuse herself from his presence. Luckily, he noted the time on his pocket watch and after a cursory nod in her direction, headed off toward the manor.

Sarah sighed with relief to have him gone. His very existence seemed to question her own and she did not like the feeling of having her life questioned. She could not help it if she was a girl with a man's job to do.

She opened the door and greeted old Zigor with a scratch behind the ear, smiling as his hind paw jogged the air. She found her father asleep in his chair, a patch of sunlight from the window lying over him like a blanket. The fireplace had gone cold, and she started a fire in anticipation of a cold night. Going into the kitchen, she surprised old Emma coming in from the back garden.

"Oh, miss! You startled me!"

"Sorry, Emma. Do you need some help?"

"No, just wanted some greens for the potatoes." She went to the pot over the fire and added something green with leaves to the pot.

Sarah rarely cooked, and could not guess what it

9

was. The only green thing she could confidently identify was hay.

Emma pottered around while Sarah got down three plates and set them at the small table. Having already cooked for the grooms, Emma would now eat her supper with Sarah and her father.

"What did the grooms have tonight?"

"Peas and ham."

"And what are we having?"

"Ham and peas."

Sarah chuckled. "And potatoes with unidentified green things."

"That's mint, missy."

"Ah. Mint."

"You should know that. You'll be needing to cook one day when you get married."

"I can't get married, Emma. I need to stay and take care of the horses. The old duke said so."

"What does the new duke say? I saw him here."

"Mmm. He disapproves of me, I fear."

"Well, it was probably something of a shock for him."

"He lived through it. Let me go call *Aitatxo*." She went down the narrow, twisting hall and found her father awake in his chair. "*Aitatxo*, dinner is ready."

"I'm coming. What happened with the horses?"

"The new duke frightened Hope and he ran off—took the fence at the far end of the ring in a single bound! Had to go fetch him from the woods."

Arnas shook his head. "There may be trouble with that one. He doesn't understand the horses."

Sarah shrugged and tucked a tendril of hair behind her ear. "Only time will tell."

Emma settled her tidy bulk into a chair and Arnas reached across to dip up his plate. "Ham and peas! English delicacy!"

"I know you would prefer some Spanish mixture."

"Basque, my dear. And yes—some *bacalao* or *ajoaerriero*, perhaps even some *kokotxas*!"

"Mmm. Well, I don't know about any of those, but a nice roast or lamb chop for me."

The two of them bantered back and forth. Emma was the closest thing she had to a mother since her own died twelve years before. Her father had married far above his station—falling in love with the daughter of a visiting earl. He'd nearly been sent back to Spain over it, but the old duke had relented and let them live in the cottage by the stables.

Her memories of her mother were vague— something about reading by the fire and attempting to sew. But she had taken after her father, and was a born horsewoman.

She remembered her father's pride when she rode her first horse at age three, instinctively understanding the intricate interplay of reins and leg pressure. From then on she had been his shadow.

Until the accident. Her father was on one of the new horses, a flighty creature who spooked easily. A young groom had swung out from a stall and startled the horse which had reared up, then toppled, crushing Arnas's leg.

He refused to let it be amputated, and instead insisted on simply having it immobilized while he rested.

And so, Sarah had filled in for her father, much to the amusement of the old duke. He had spent hours in the stables, slowly allowing Sarah to have more rein and say in the management of the horses. Even when Arnas's leg had been strong enough for him to hobble about the yard, Sarah's voice still carried weight.

The truth was, Arnas could do very little. Reliant upon his cane, each step was arduous and painful. Most of the time he sat in the sunshine, watching from his stoop and shouting orders across the yard.

"The funeral for the old duke will be in a few days," Emma said.

"Will any of the horses be involved?" Sarah asked.

"No. He will be interred in the chapel. No procession."

"So business as usual for us."

Her father nodded. "We will have a lot of extra horses and carriages to house, not to mention grooms and drivers. We'll have to double up."

"Emma can stay with me like always. You needn't double, *Aitatxo*."

"Gordon, the driver, can bunk with me. We'll need his bed for two of the others, and I would rather someone I know than someone I don't."

She sighed. "Hopefully this will pass soon enough."

"It will."

Rising to go to her room, she thought for a moment. Once there, she pulled out one of her three dresses. She had worn it not too long ago, and it still fit…if a little short.

Like the others, it was a muslin drop front dress, this one nearly white while of the others, one was faded blue and the other dark green.

Perhaps, she should start wearing her dresses every

day. But then that would mean the sidesaddle with all its idiosyncrasies, and she shook her head.

The new duke would just have to take her as she was!

Chapter Three

The morning of the funeral dawned foggy and damp. William rose and pulled his dressing gown around him to go down to breakfast. All through the manor, hushed sounds of movement echoed as people worked to get ready for the event. He quickly dished up a plate and ate his eggs and tomatoes while sipping the coffee—more fortifying than tea. He was the only one down, so far.

Withcombe. He stared around him at the paintings and plasterwork, the wainscot and arched doorways. As a child he had run happily enough through its halls and rooms. Until called to order by his father...

He finished eating and set his napkin down beside his plate before returning to his room. By the time he reached it, his valet had pulled his mourning suit out and brushed it thoroughly. It took some time to get shaved and his hair combed into submission. Then the clothes, cravat, boots. Finally, he stood surveying his appearance in the long mirror.

Tall, like his father and grandfather, broadly built like his mother's father. The black coat set off his shoulders well while the breeches hugged his slim hips. It was in his face that he saw his mother.

He sighed and turned away. As a child he had been sensitive to his mother's moods and tearful interludes, but as an adult he saw them as attempts to get attention from his father. There was a knock on the door and his mother entered, wearing her dress of black bombazine with its beaded lace and the strings of jet around her neck.

"Ah. You're ready. We will need to join our guests in the west parlor before going down to the chapel. Are you ready to take your place in the duke's bedchamber?"

He frowned. "He's not even in the ground yet…"

"But he will be. I ordered the servants to get it ready for you."

"Mother…I am content where I am."

"It will be easiest on the servants if things are not changed from their usual routine."

"I can't see how me staying in the Vineyard Room will upset the servants." He looked at the grape leaves embroidered on the counterpane which gave the room its name. "I've always been comfortable here."

"All three times you visited."

"You forget, I grew up here. I am quite familiar with Withcombe."

She pursed her lined lips. "Well, come down, then."

"In a moment."

He waited for her to leave and sat down on the window seat. Below, a line of carriages discharged their passengers to join the mourners. He sighed, and rose to do his duty.

It wasn't until later, in the pew listening to the archbishop deliver the funeral mass, that he reflected that he was truly the heir and that the upkeep of Withcombe would be his responsibility. He stared at the box that contained his father's mortal remains and felt sorrow for the first time since his father had died. But it was sorrow for what was never to be.

His own man in his own world.

Hours later, the last guest had left and he carried a glass of brandy up to his room. He opened the door to the Vineyard Room, only to find the bed stripped with the counterpane folded at the foot of the bed. He heard a sound behind him and spun to find Larkin, his valet.

"Ah, Duke Tensington, your things have been moved by order of the duchess."

"Indeed. And where have they been moved?"

"To the duke's room, your grace."

He closed his eyes and breathed for a moment, before striding off toward what had been his father's room. He had to cross to the east wing, near where his own room had been as a child. Two doors down was the Duke's Room as it had always been called. He paused outside the doors, then pushed them in slowly.

It looked much the same as it always had done. Red velvet bedspread and crimson jacquard bed curtains. The red reminded him of blood, which brought to mind his accident all those years ago. He banished the thought from his mind, but not before a nugget of disquiet lodged itself in his heart. Surely, nothing good would come of his taking his father's room.

He glanced around, but only Larkin was there, going through a drawer and pulling out a nightshirt, then arranging his brushes on the dressing table. He felt defeated; his mother had won.

Slowly, he walked around the room. His father's old riding crop stood in a corner and he picked it up. He would never be the horseman his father was. He tapped the crop against his palm and looked around before setting it back down. Over the fireplace was the painting his father had commissioned of Tunbridge Blue's father—Tunbridge Oak. The dark bay's long lines were exaggerated, the painting imbuing the long-dead horse with far more elegance than he'd had in life. His blood boiled that his father had kept this painting, of this particular horse, in his bedroom.

He strode to the bell cord and pulled it. When the footman arrived, he pointed to the painting. "That comes down tonight. Get whatever help you need, but get it out of here now."

The bewildered servant nodded and ran off. It took nearly an hour for them to find a ladder that would reach. When the footman tried to unhook it, the painting fell and hit the stone hearth, cracking the wood frame.

All stared at William but he simply gestured toward the painting. "Throw it out. I don't want to see it ever again."

Startled glances were shot to one another, but they quickly cleaned up the space and left William alone in the room. A moment after they had gone, his mother floated in.

"Whatever has been going on?"

William shrugged. "Just a little housecleaning."

She glanced around. "You should have the bed curtains changed."

"I plan to have the whole room redone. Counterpane, curtains, the lot."

"The horse painting is gone."

"Yes," he said grimly.

"What shall you put in its place?"

"I don't know. I shall have to think on it. Maybe

the small portrait of the first duke."

"Mmm, appropriate. I shall begin preparing to go to the Dower House."

"Mother, you don't need to leave your home."

"This has never been my home. For years now I have looked forward to Marwinne."

She exited the room with a sweep of her dressing gown, leaving William alone in the room where his father had lived, and died.

Chapter Four

Sarah finished eating and carried her plate to the sink. She pulled on an overcoat to ward off the chill of the evening and went about the rounds.

"Make sure you check on Hope—that he is sound after his adventure. And Poppy was looking near ready to foal."

"Yes, *Aitatxo*." She stepped out into the cool air and headed for the stables.

The old duke had been buried these past few weeks, and life had carried on much as usual. The new duke had stayed away for the most part, something Sarah was grateful for.

The first stall, with its placard hanging over the door, was that of Tunbridge Blue, a big, dark bay that was nearly black. He had been the pride of Withcombe. Sarah frowned, for he wasn't alone.

The new duke stood, hands in pockets, staring at the old stallion. Sarah cleared her throat and he spun.

"Ah. Just thought I'd come down and see what I'm spending my money on."

"Your father thought they were important."

"Yes, but I have to balance the finances of the estate now. Trying to understand everything that goes into this endeavor."

"Withcombe Bays are famous—"

"Not as much as they were. Bay horses are rather

out of fashion, just now. Black and dapple gray are in."

"Fashions change."

"Yes, but perhaps it would make sense to lighten the load on the stables until they changed back. Or get in some horses that are more in fashion."

She stared at him and he frowned. The sheer ignorance of such a statement!

"It takes almost a year for a foal to be born, then six months until it is weaned. Then growing and training—years are invested into a single horse. By then, the fashions will have changed."

"Then maybe branch out."

"We are known for our bays!"

"I. It is my estate now. Withcombe is me."

"And what about the lot of us slaving away in the shadows?"

"I pity your predicament, but the burden of responsibility for Withcombe is on me." He glanced over at Blue. "And that starts with questioning things like keeping an old horse that is unable to perform, as you said."

Her eyes flew wide. "You can't be serious! Blue is the greatest horse I have ever known! He has earned his time in pasture!"

"And yet, here he is taking up a stall. I'm sure grooms and whatnot are used for his upkeep. Hay, oats, other things. All these things could be going to a productive horse."

Her mouth dropped open. "We are getting him ready for the pasture. One isn't available just yet. Broodmares are out there."

He shrugged and moved onto the next stall. "And who is this?"

"Bard. He is a gelding. A great hunter."

"I have a hunter—where is he?"

"The gray? We have him over in the barn."

"I want him switched with this horse."

"But—"

"Here," he called to a passing groom. "Fetch my hunter. He's the dapple gray in the barn. Bring him here and take this horse over to the barn."

The groom's gaze slid to Sarah, who stared stonily down. "M-miss?" His voice wavered.

"I am Duke of Tensington, Withcombe is my estate. I say move the horses."

The groom turned, with a final look at Sarah and headed off toward the barn.

"Any other changes, your grace?" Her voice sounded taut, even to her ears.

He stretched and blew out a breath. "Not right now. But I will certainly be far more involved than I have been." He nodded at her and headed up the rise to the manor house.

She'd had to battle hard enough as it was to gain respect of the grooms and stable boys, and now this new duke had undermined it all in one mindless exercise of control.

She hated him.

Hate was not too strong a word for the emotions swirling through her at the moment. She turned a little shakily and headed back toward the cottage. She could see her father's face in the window, and she shuddered.

"What is going on? I saw the duke talking to you. Why do you look like that?"

"He wants to sell Blue, and insisted we put his own horse in Bard's stall."

Arnas turned an unseemly shade of red, one hand clenching and unclenching. "Why does he not leave all this to us?"

"He wanted to make a point, which is that this is his place, and he is in charge. I am sure of it."

"But he knows nothing of horses! I do not think he even likes them."

Sarah shrugged. The rage had triggered tears of frustration, and she fought against them. She sniffed and her father reached out.

"Never mind, *Potxola*. I will go talk to him."

Her voice broke. "How, *Aitatxo*? You cannot walk."

"I will take the pony cart, with old Pudge."

"You should take Bard."

He laughed. "Ha! Maybe I will."

"I should go, too."

He was silent for a moment, considering. "Yes, perhaps you should. You and I and Bard will go see if we can talk some sense into our new duke."

The next morning, Sarah came down the stairs, holding herself rather awkwardly. Her fine corset was a little stiffer than the one she normally wore. Her dress had a tiny repair near the hem which she hoped no one would see, and her boots peeked out from under the hem of the dress that was a year's growth too short.

Emma took one look at her, moved the kettle off the fire, then motioned her back upstairs.

Sarah sighed, and plodded back to her room. She sat at the tiny dressing table and stared into the mirror. Emma brushed her hair out and teased it into fullness, then up into a fancy twist with tendrils hanging down. She dug in the box of Sarah's mother's things and found a curling iron which she quickly cleaned, then heated in the little fireplace and used to curl the tendrils around her face.

Sarah looked at her reflection, barely recognizing herself. Gone was the messy braid coiled into a roll on the back of her head. Instead, she looked elegant, almost, like any other girl she had seen.

Emma dug through the box and pulled out a roll of some satin material. "Ah, one of your mother's sashes." She used the iron to smooth out the wrinkles and bid Sarah stand. She tied it around the simple gathered skirt of her plain linen dress. "Do you have any of your mother's jewelry?"

Sarah huffed, but opened a drawer and took out a few boxes. Emma went through them all, then chose a necklace of tiny pearls and simple gold earrings. Then she turned her attention to Sarah's feet and said, "You cannot wear those boots with this dress. You must have some slippers around…"

"Ummm…Maybe under my bed?"

Emma sighed and lowered her bulk to peer under the bed. Then, with a happy cry, she reached underneath and pulled free a pair of relatively clean leather slippers. She wet a corner of her apron and wiped a mark from one of the shoes then set them on the ground, as Sarah struggled out of her work boots. Sarah slipped them on and stood, then twirled around.

"Will I do?"

Emma grinned. "Aye, you'll do."

Sarah trotted down the stairs and out, where her father sat in the old cart holding the reins. She climbed up onto the box beside him and he chirruped to Bard who set off.

Chapter Five

William sat listening to his house guest, Magdalene Umphert, the Marchioness of Lilsbury, or Maggie as he called her. Her clear, somewhat nasal tones dripped with sarcasm as she discussed one of her favorite topics—other women's shortcomings.

"Oh, my dear, if you had only seen her: tall, yes, but so gangly as to look freakish. Last year's gown and I can't tell you how old the slippers were. Luckily I only saw the tips of them. But honestly, dressed like that in front of Pembley—none of us knew where to look."

William stifled a yawn. "Is Pembley interested in her?"

"Well I should say not. He hardly looked at her. Who would? Poor dear." But a cat-like smile played around her mouth.

"Well, Maggie, we can't help how we look…"

"To some degree, I agree with you. But a little sense in dressing goes a long way."

"I've heard you accuse her of no more than being out of date, fashion-wise."

"In my circle, that's enough."

The butler appeared at the arched entrance to the parlor. "Excuse me, your grace, but there is a *person* to see you."

William chuckled into his hand. "Jarvis, what do

you mean? What sort of person?"

"A horse person. A Mr. Mondragón."

"Ah!" He looked over at Maggie, "I know what this is about."

"Shall I go upstairs?"

"No, no. Stay a bit." He motioned for Jarvis to bring in his visitor. After a few minutes, he looked up to see Arnas and a lovely young girl at his side. It wasn't until the girl turned hard eyes upon him that he recognized Sarah Mondragón. Suddenly, he wished he had sent Maggie away.

"Mondragón. If this is about the horses…"

"But of course it is about the horses, your grace. I am not qualified to speak on any other topic."

"My decision stands. I want my horse in the stables."

"I understand. What my daughter did not explain to you was that your horse has weak lungs, and the stables are exposed to the damp, cold air from the fells. In the barn, he is protected from such."

"What are you saying? My horse has bad lungs?"

"Not bad, but not robust as Withcombe Bard who usually occupies that stall. He was, after all, bred here in this country."

Maggie smiled and lifted her chin. "Really, old man, I should think you ashamed to lecture his grace about his horse."

But William remembered the mild cough he had heard after his only ride and frowned. He was suddenly unsure of himself, and the sensation unsettled him. He hushed Maggie with a hand, and dragged his gaze from Sarah to stare at her father.

"Perhaps I acted out of turn. I want my horses

cared for in the best possible manner."

Sarah spoke for the first time. "That is what we all want."

William looked at her and nodded. "We agree there, at least." He waved them off. "Put my horse back in the barn, then. But don't be surprised if I come round questioning your decisions. I will be looking into the finances of the stables very carefully."

"Of course," said Arnas.

He bowed and flicked Sarah with the back of his hand. She dropped a creditable curtsey and stalked from the room, with her father in tow.

They had barely left when Maggie burst out in laughter. "Oh my dear, thank you for letting me stay! Good Lord, how fun! Do you know I find it amusing to see poor girls try to dress up. The things they put together! Twenty-year-old sash, five-year-old dress, and pearls! Oh my goodness!"

William frowned. It may be as Maggie said, but he could not help but think Sarah had looked rather fine. Suddenly he was more than ready for his houseguest to be gone.

"Ah! So what shall we do for the next two weeks? I know—a hunt!"

William sighed, eyebrows raised. He was no huntsman…"Or…a ball?"

Maggie clapped her delicate hands. "Oh, that would be wonderful. Do let's have a ball."

He breathed a sigh of relief. "I'll get Hinckley to sort it all out."

He rang the bell and ordered the footman who appeared to fetch the housekeeper. After a few minutes, a stately matron dressed all in dark gray appeared, her chatelaine dangling from her waist.

"Yes, Duke Tensington?" Hinckley said.

"We are having a ball. How soon can one be organized?"

"A week, at least, your grace."

"Excellent. The usual families, etc."

"I would be happy to consult on menu, music, and dances," Maggie said.

Hinckley bowed her head in her direction, then looked back at the duke. "Is that all, your grace?"

"Yes, Hinckley." The housekeeper turned and glided serenely away while Maggie went to the pianoforte.

"You're going to play?"

"I must practice. You said earlier that the Bonnigams and Wolfhardts would be coming to dinner. I shall have to play something."

A round little woman bustled into the room. It was Mildred Poppingham, Maggie's spinster cousin and chaperone. Her large bust balanced above her tummy, covered with a filmy chemise. She set her shawl down on the settee and went to the tea service to pour herself a cup of tea. Her mouth puckered into a *moue* of distaste after the first sip.

"Ah. Cold. But I was delayed coming down due to a letter I received. Our dearest Magdalene's newest horse has been delivered."

"Maggie, you should have bought one of mine. I have an estate full now."

Maggie's fingers flew over the keys in a warming up sequence and she smiled. "You didn't when I was in need of one. No harm done—one horse is pretty much like the rest."

"Don't let my horsemaster hear you…"

Maggie began to play in earnest, and he wondered again at his imperturbability where she was concerned. She was pretty—beautiful even—with golden hair and blue eyes set off by dark lashes. She could play and sing, and look lovely while doing so. And yet, he was unmoved. They were simply old friends.

The mention of horses brought his own dapple gray hunter to mind. He'd only ridden the once, usually managing to take the carriage rather than go anywhere on horseback. He had imported the horse from Ireland, in part to spite his father, who had shrugged it off with a simple, "You will most likely regret it."

He was most certainly not going to regret it. Arnas's mention of the horse's lungs bothered him, however. He would be unable to go the distance required of a hunter if his lungs were bad…not that he'd be given much of a chance. William tended to avoid horsey things like hunts…

Blowing out a breath, he leaned back. His mind went back to the things Maggie had said of Sarah's dress. He was almost certain the girl heard it, and it bothered him. Without thinking, he stood, and Maggie abruptly stopped playing.

"Please, continue. I'll be back shortly."

He strode from the parlor, and the sounds of the piano playing reached him as he went through the front doors and headed down to the stables.

Chapter Six

Sarah and her father were barely out of the parlor
when laughter broke out behind them. She recognized
the woman's voice, heard her say something about a
"dress", and deduced that the woman was laughing at
her. Her cheeks heated and she gritted her teeth. Tears
born of anger pricked her eyes but she blinked them
back. She would not show emotion in this place.

She did not look around, instead keeping her gaze
trained on the butler's back. She noted his collar was
precisely arranged and that his coat was completely free
of any lint. The house smelled of polish and flowers,
and…damp? Her nose wrinkled a little and her chin
lifted.

Soon enough they were out in front. A footman
helped her into the cart and startled, she thanked him.
Her father chirruped to Bard and they set off back to the
house. The day was fine, if a little cloudy, and she lifted
her face to the breeze. Though she could still hear the
marchioness's laughter in her ears, she could also smell
the stables they were nearing, and she smiled.

A stable boy came forward and took control of
Bard as they pulled up to the cottage stoop.

"Here, John, put Bard back in his stall and put the
gray back in the barn," Arnas shouted to the boy.

Sarah helped her father down, and into his chair on
the stoop before heading inside to change into work

clothes. "Emma! I'm back. Come help me out of these infernal stays!"

"Just a moment, I'm putting the kettle on. There." She appeared in Sarah's bedchamber, rubbing her hands on her apron. "All right, let's get you out of these clothes, though it does my eyes good to see you dressed like this."

"Well, they just laughed at me."

"That's on them. You did your best and that's all you can do." The dress dropped into a pile at Sarah's feet as Emma then pulled the strings of the corset loose. "There. Do you need help getting dressed?"

Sarah chuckled. "No, I do this every day."

"You should really think about getting another dress or two made. I can write my sister. She lives in Wexley."

Sarah stilled. "I suppose…in case I need to go out again."

Emma smiled and picked up the forgotten dress. "Oh, here, let me undo those pearls for you."

Sarah bent her neck, then took the pearls and replaced them in their box.

"Thank you, Em."

Emma patted her cheek and bustled out. Sarah sat at her dressing table for a moment, looking at her hair and how the earrings glinted through the curling tendrils. The image in the mirror was foreign, to her eyes, but she liked it and wondered if she should spend a little more time on her appearance now and then. She sighed and pushed up from the table.

Old corset, work pants and oversized shirt. She had a time tucking it in all around before tying the belt. Then she had to pull on her working boots before clomping down the stairs.

Her father was in the yard barking orders at the grooms. She patted his beret and went first to the old stallion, Blue. John, the head groom, met her and stood with hands behind his back.

"Anything I need to know about?"

"'Ol Blue didn't like the gray and tried to bite him, ended up banging his chin on the divider and has a lump now. We put a poultice on it so it won't abscess."

Sarah stroked the dark nose that whuffled at her over the door. She felt under his jaw and found the swelling. It was not large and the poultice seemed to be doing its job. Nodding, she gave him a final pat and moved on to Bard who was a little unsettled in his stall. One by one, they went through the horses, with Arnas shouting questions now and then. When they had finished the square of stalls, they made their way to the barn and did the same for the horses out there. Then they went from pasture to pasture, looking at the mares out in the fields.

Sarah pointed to one of the mares. Her belly hung low and the space in front of her hips seemed hollowed out.

"Poppy's dropped. Have her brought into the foaling box."

Her gaze scanned the rest and she found another to be brought in. John snapped his fingers to a pair of stable boys and spoke tersely to each. They scuttled off in search of lead ropes and halters.

The gong rang, and soon boys were appearing from everywhere, like rats from a sinking ship. They all converged on the kitchen area and picked up their plate with stew and a slice of bread. Soon the courtyard was silent, save for the scrape of spoons against the pewter plates. Two maids stood ready at the wash basins to clean the used plates and spoons coming back. Sarah collected her father's plate, then took it and her own in and handed it to sour-faced Edith, who accepted it without looking at her.

The clouds had congregated, but the rain held off and she went to Hope's stall to look him over. She called to a groom to lead him out and he walked in a circle around her. Each step was firm, and he even bounced a little on his toes as he went. She breathed a sigh of relief that he hadn't been injured.

The courtyard went silent, and Hope lifted his head, snatching at the lead. She grabbed it from the groom. With a measured voice, she calmed the horse, then turned to look.

The duke stood there, watching.

"Your grace?"

"Please, carry on. Is he all right from his adventure?"

She nodded, but looked away quickly. "Yes, he seems fine."

He stepped closer, then paused. "I used to come down here with my father."

"Oh yes?"

"Did you think about how we can bring more colors in our horses?"

"The problem is, our base stock is Cleveland Bays. They tend to be…bay. We breed in Thoroughbred from time to time, but the colors rarely come through."

He stepped a little closer. "Could we bring in some more Thoroughbreds?"

She frowned, "We could, but…"

"But?"

She nodded toward Hope. "He is half Thoroughbred, and very highly strung. He will calm in time, but it is not a character one wants in carriage horses or hunters."

"So why do we have him if his character is not the best?"

She reached up and stroked the light bay face. He bent his neck and nuzzled her shoulder, lipping her blouse and then nodding his head. Grinning, she turned to the duke, and his eyes widened suddenly.

"See, he has a wonderful character. And his lines and conformation are the best we've seen in a long time. He will bring elegance to our stable. Come, touch him."

The duke frowned, but edged closer. He stretched out a hand, and Hope bobbed his nose back and forth a few times, then stopped, nostrils flaring as he sniffed the proffered hand. Then Hope took a step closer and the duke's fingers cupped his chin.

"I don't think I've touched a horse apart from occasionally riding since I was a child."

"Why did you stop coming to the stables?"

He blew out a breath. "That's a long, unpleasant story. Never mind." He pulled his hand back and Hope snatched his head away. "I came to apologize for the marchioness's comments."

Sarah silently cursed her suddenly flaming cheeks and looked away. "No apology needed. I'm sorry if I embarrassed you."

"No. I mean, you were…no. Please don't concern yourself with that."

"No, I won't. Was there something else?"

He stiffened. "No, Miss Mondragón." He turned, then paused and added, "But I think we should meet regularly to discuss the horses."

"As you wish, your grace."

She watched him walk away and wondered what he would look like riding a horse. That he was almost afraid of them was obvious—but why?

"*Aitatxo*?" She called across the courtyard, then she handed Hope off to a groom with orders to walk him.

"Yes?"

She strode up to her father and paused beside him. "*Aitatxo*, do you know what happened with the duke?"

"You mean why he doesn't care so much for the horses?"

"Yes, exactly."

"Hmm. I do, but I think he should tell you. Just keep doing what you are doing. It will help him." He looked at her. "It is important that he come to love the horses like his father. All this we have worked for depends upon it."

She nodded, and glanced up to see the duke disappearing up the rise toward the manor. A little sorrow welled up within her, a sadness at a life spent in fear of the animals she loved. What had happened to turn him?

For now, though, she had two mares in the foaling boxes to inspect. Sarah made her way to the far end of the stable quad and peered over the door at the first one. Poppy was the first foal she had assisted with, and was special to her. She had supervised her breeding—one of the last to old Blue, and now waited to see what Poppy's first foal would be.

She lifted the latch and went into the box. The mare watched her approach, ears up and forward. Sarah laid a hand on the warm neck, then let it slide down until it rested on the large mound of her belly. She let her hands press and gauge the position of the foal. It moved, kicking strong, and she smiled. It was a big foal, as Blue's offspring often were, and the mare a little on the slight side. Sarah bit her lip, hoping all would be well.

The other mare was nervous, and lumbered away from her pressing hands so she stopped rather than make her anxious. As she stood outside the boxes, she looked down at her clothes—castoff pants and shirt from her father. There was little to distinguish her from the other stable boys and grooms. Her father and Emma had prevailed upon her to dress appropriately, but she had resisted.

Perhaps they were right.

Sarah considered what she had to wear. Only three dresses, two of which were dark so they would not show stains all that badly. She wore them to church every Sunday, but often with her boots underneath. She wondered if the new duke went to church in his manor on the hill. She stopped and frowned...why did she care what the new duke did?

She stood and left the foaling box to go check on the horses in the barn.

****

Morning pierced her little window and Sarah stirred under her covers. Then she sat up. She could hear the boys out in the courtyard, feeding and watering and going about the day. Stretching a little, she yawned and then swung her legs out of bed to get dressed.

It was slow going; her good corset was more difficult to handle without help, and she fumbled with the buttons of the dark green, drop-front gown. Then she went through the trunk at the end of her bed that contained her mother's old clothes. She rooted around until she found her apron, the black one that slipped on from the front. Her mother had often worn it when going around with Arnas to look at the horses. It was wrinkled from years in the chest, but she slipped it on and then pulled on her boots. Looking at herself in the mirror, she flashed her eyebrows and grinned at what the boys would say to see her in a dress.

Emma did a double-take and smiled. "Oh, it does my heart good to see you so!"

Zigor and Arnas appeared at the door to the little nook where they ate. "Humph. All dressed up with nowhere to go."

"I have plenty of places to go, *Aitatxo*. The whole stables and pastures…everywhere."

He smiled and patted her cheek.

They ate their breakfast. Then Sarah sprang up to help with the dishes before running outside. The sunrise had promised sunshine, but clouds had spread in from the east. She headed first to the old stallion's stall and noted he was out being groomed while his stall was cleaned. She went along, checking that everything was being done as it should be. One by one the boys shot her second looks and she chuckled to herself. Finally, she came to Hope's stall. He bobbed his head out and nickered softly.

She stroked the offered nose and scratched him under his jaw. He stretched out his neck and his eyes closed.

"He seems to be enjoying that!"

Sarah jumped, startling the horse, who bolted to the opposite side of the stall and squealed. She spun to see the duke standing there, dressed in riding breeches and a brown coat.

"Your grace!"

"It's Duke Tensington the first time, then your grace."

"I apologize, Duke Tensington."

"Not at all. I called for my horse and the Marchioness of Lilsbury's to be saddled and readied."

"Of course. We would have brought them to the manor house."

She glanced away. The dapple gray and the black were being led up from the barn.

"I felt like walking down. I always seem to disturb this fellow."

"Yes." She took a few steps and stood looking at Poppy, who came calmly over and popped her head over the door. She reached her arms around the warm neck and breathed in her sweet scent.

"You really love them. Don't you?"

She nodded, then pulled slowly back. "Why don't you?"

He shrugged. "I did as a boy, but...well. They sort of fell out of favor with me."

"What happened?"

He reached out a tentative hand and stroked the brown neck. "I had a bad accident with one—Blue's sire actually. My father insisted I ride him and I fell, but he dragged me for some ways. Ended up bedridden for weeks and my mother insisted I stay away from them for my own safety. Difficult to give them up completely, however. Eventually I was forced to ride a bit. But, I'm no horseman."

"You could be. It is never too late to learn."

He chuckled. "And what would you have me do first?"

Thinking back to the awkward seat he'd had when he had ridden to help with Hope, she said, "Well, first we would work on your balance. Then your reining, and I imagine your jumping is unsightly."

"I manage to stay on, but only just. All right, if you can teach me how to ride to Hunt, then I'll agree we can keep the old stallion."

Her mouth dropped open. "Yes! Oh yes! When shall we start?"

He glanced over as his horse was brought up to him. "How about now?"

"Isn't your guest waiting?"

"She is likely entertained. A short lesson, then."

She crossed her arms. "Right then. Mount." She watched him haul himself up with a critical eye. "That will need to improve. Cup your hips forward a bit more…there. Now stick your arms out."

"What, like this?"

"Exactly. Now stay like that."

She took the lead from the groom and led the horse forward. The duke bobbed side to side with each step, then after a while, managed to hold himself straight as the horse stepped.

"There, doesn't that feel better?"

He nodded. "I think so. I can feel a difference."

"Whatever you are doing on the horse, look for that balance." She handed him the reins. "Lesson one is over."

He smiled down at her, tipped his hat, then rode away with only a slight wobble.

Chapter Seven

William rode up to the house, ever mindful of his seat and the little core inside that seemed to tell him when he was balanced. It seemed to bob all about, though less and less as time passed. He and the marchioness's horse arrived at the manor and the butler disappeared to call her.

As she swept out in a deep blue riding habit and matching hat, he thought again of Sarah's dark green dress and black apron, and her boots peeking out from underneath…and smiled.

"Ah, there you are, you naughty boy. Where were you?"

"I went to get the horses. Here I am."

He watched as she was helped up onto her horse. She took a long moment to arrange her dress just so, and then nodded genteelly to him. He scanned his memory of Withcombe's grounds for somewhere interesting to ride, and decided to take her down through the little wood where Hope had run to.

They set off, William mindful of his seat and working hard to keep his balance. Maggie cantered ahead a little and he wondered how women rode sidesaddle. Sarah Mondragón doesn't…

He pushed his horse into a canter to catch up and they rode shoulder to shoulder for a time until they came to the woods. There was a track going through, and he guided his horse into it. Maggie followed as the tree branches formed a roof overhead.

Shadows spread around them, sunlight piercing through from time to time. He came to the little clearing where Hope had been found and pulled up.

"This is where we found the new stallion after he had run off."

"I can't believe your horse person let him do that."

"Well, I did startle him."

"Then he isn't well trained. Horses shouldn't run off."

"Well, but they do. Sometimes."

"Handler mistakes, usually. I would have sacked the man then and there."

"Woman."

"What?"

"It was a woman—the old horsemaster's daughter." He instantly regretted his words.

Maggie stared at him. "You have a woman, a young woman...wait a moment. That girl...that girl that came with the horse man yesterday."

"Um...yes."

"You cannot allow it! It's indecent! A woman should not be in control of such things...Think what she is exposed to! Stallions and mares, and...other distasteful things."

William frowned. "I don't know how distasteful it all is. She is certainly used to it. Second nature so to speak."

"Good God, no wonder she didn't know how to dress."

Irritation roiled suddenly in William. He did not like the way the conversation had gone. "Well, you don't need to worry about it." He reined his horse around and headed off, leaving her to follow.

She was silent for a few minutes, until they exited the woods. "I don't understand your attitude toward this horse girl. For her own sake she should be sacked."

"And then what? Where would they go? The father is crippled, my father valued them…"

"Your father was an old dear to keep them, but still. I know a man who would be perfect for your stables. Bring some new blood in and make them what they once were."

"We still manage to sell all of our horses we put up. And we have a list of future buyers."

"Well, I am only a woman, but I have some sense according to my friends. I am appalled that you are keeping this girl."

William blew out a breath. "Let's talk of other things. Didn't you say you were getting a new pianoforte?"

"Yes! It is perfectly lovely. It is so well suited to my east parlor, and the gilt catches the light as it comes in through the windows."

"Sounds perfect."

"It is. Unfortunately it needs to be tuned, but then I plan to have a large house party. You'll simply have to come!"

"I will be happy to."

They managed the rest of their ride without any further arguments, for which William was grateful. By the time they pulled up at the front steps of the manor house, he was more than ready to get down and eat a late luncheon. Maggie had talked mostly non-stop, and his ears were actually ringing.

"Please, excuse me," he said as he slid down from the back of his horse. "I must go check on the progress of supper. If you would join me in the dining room I'll see that we have a light luncheon."

"Oh, I never take luncheon. Perhaps a little tea and a small sandwich or two."

"Of course. I will arrange it." He strode off to find a servant to convey his orders to. Once he had done so, he trotted up the sweeping staircase to his room.

He quickly divested himself of his riding clothes and changed into what his valet had pulled out for him. He batted Larkin's hands from his trousers, but let him help with tying the cravat and holding his jacket.

The parlor was empty when he entered. He went to the dining room where a light luncheon of a tray of sliced sandwiches, and a cold salad had been set. An arrangement of fresh fruit acted as the centerpiece. The marchioness lifted her chin in his direction, took a sip of tea, then a bite of sandwich.

"Your staff does these quite well."

"I simply inherited them."

"Well, don't change them. Someone did an excellent job hiring them."

"Probably my mother."

"Where is she?"

"She insisted on moving to Marwinne. It has traditionally acted as the dower house."

"Lucky you not to have your mother underfoot. Mine sits in her parlor embroidering things of indeterminate use. As though I need or want a hand-embroidered reticule!"

"At least she keeps busy."

"Yes, there's that. What are your plans for

Withcombe?"

He lifted one shoulder. "I don't really have plans as yet. I am still going over the accounts and learning my way around."

"I take it the estate is solvent?"

"So far. The farms produce well; horse sales are down, but steady. Several offers for Tunbridge Blue, but the Mondragóns are resistant to selling him."

"What does it matter? It is your horse."

"Yes…well, I am still considering what is best." He did not know why the marchioness's words should irritate him so. He frowned to himself.

"And what is that look for?"

"Nothing. Will you play after luncheon?"

She leaned back against the chair and sighed. "I am unaccountably tired today. I may just lie down in my room."

For some reason, this news filled him with relief. His mind shot suddenly to the stables, and he wondered if he should go down to check on things. After laying his napkin down on the table, he rose and headed out the door.

The clouds overhead pressed down upon the earth, promising a storm to come. He grabbed an umbrella before setting off. The walk down to the stables seemed to go faster with each venture, and within minutes he stood at the entrance to the quad, with Tunbridge Blue looking at him with large brown eyes. He stopped a passing groom.

"Where is Miss Mondragón?"

He pointed to the far end of the rectangle. "She is with one of the broodmares."

William headed off in the direction he had

indicated, horses' heads bobbing out the door to look at him as he passed. He paused to stroke Hope's velvety nose, then hurried on.

He found Sarah standing at the door to Poppy's stall. She turned a worried face to him.

He frowned. "What's wrong?"

She pointed to the mare with her chin. Poppy would take a few steps around the stall, then stop and strain. Now and then tiny hooves appeared at her vulva, then disappeared back inside.

"She has been like this for too long. The foal is stuck."

With a heavy grunt, the horse lay down and continued to strain, her legs lifting off the ground with the force of her pushing. Sarah opened the door and went in.

"What are you doing?"

"I have to get this foal out of her."

She pushed up her sleeves and reached inside the horse, feeling around. Her grip strengthened and she pulled with the horse's contraction. Two hooves and a nose appeared. They almost disappeared when the contraction was over.

"Progress. Here, come help me."

Startled, William drew back. "What?"

"I need help; come pull with me."

Slowly, he removed his jacket and waistcoat and set them over the side of the stall. Then he stepped uncertainly in. "Now what?"

"Kneel down here beside me; grab on to one of the hooves and maintain traction."

William knelt beside her, his thigh touching hers and feeling her warmth. She smelled of hay and horses and…roses? Cautiously he reached out toward the horse. Sarah quickly grasped his hands with one of hers and drew them toward one of the hooves.

It was warm, and slippery, and he recoiled with disgust at first. He glanced over at Sarah, her face reddened with exertion. He tightened his grip, and pulled.

The horse stiffened with another contraction, and this time more than the little nose appeared. Shoulder to shoulder, hip to hip, they battled to pull the foal free of its mother. William felt a thrill as more and more of the foal showed with each contraction. With a sudden rush, the foal's shoulders appeared, and with two more contractions, the foal fell into their laps, kicking.

Sarah quickly removed the membranes from the baby's face and wiped the mucus from its nose. Then she pushed it towards Poppy's head and sat back, wiping her hands on the straw, and then her apron. She lifted a shining face to William and without thinking, he bent to kiss her.

Her eyes flew wide and she jumped away, one hand going to her mouth where his lips had barely brushed. She stood roughly, and he followed, effectively blocking her from the door. He held out a hand to her. "Please forgive me."

"I…of course. We should leave her to it."

"Yes." He fumbled with the door's latch and opened it.

She followed him and all but ran away, moving ever faster, as she headed toward her home.

"Damn it!" he swore.

Chapter Eight

Sarah all but ran home in a daze. She did not see the grooms and stable boys she passed, nor did she pause to speak to her father on the stoop. Instead she sprinted upstairs to her room and stood there, shaking.

A kiss? He had kissed her! A real kiss—his lips had touched hers. She had rarely even seen kissing, except long ago when her father used to kiss her mother. She had dreamed of it, of course. Nameless, faceless men who pressed their mouths against hers…nothing like the gentle touch of the duke's lips.

The fluids from the foal's birth were drying and cooling. She quickly undressed and washed in her basin. The cold water helped waken her from her stupor. She pulled on her other dark dress and hunted through the trunk for another apron—this one light beige. She scooped up her dirty clothes and carried them downstairs to the laundry room.

Her father sat in his chair. "Sarah, come here. Who foaled?"

"Poppy. I had to help her."

"What did she have?"

"I…I don't know."

"You didn't check?"

"No. I'll go do so now."

She ran from her father, closed the front door behind her and looked around to make sure the duke was gone. When she was assured he was, she trotted toward the broodmare's stalls and peered over the door at Poppy and her baby. It was tottering on long legs and working its way toward her udder. Sarah hung over the door for a few minutes, waiting to see it begin to nurse.

She unlatched the door and stepped in. She stroked the damp fur of the foal and peeked underneath to see that it was a boy. Poppy had given them a colt. Glancing around, she caught sight of a stable lad and called him over.

"Spread some fresh straw in here and bring her a warm mash."

"Yes, miss." He shot off.

With her feet moving by themselves, she made her way toward the end of the row of stalls. She passed Hope's door, to find him looking out at the world with curious eyes. She patted his neck and went past until she reached Blue. He ambled over to her and ducked his head over the door.

Stroking his nose and scratching under his chin, she said, "Another colt, Blue. Another star, I'm sure."

He lipped her fingers and she smiled, cupping his chin in her hands and laying her cheek against his nose. He pulled free and she let him go, watching as he touched noses with Bard next door, then strolled over to his hay box.

She made her way back to the house. Arnas was waiting for her.

"Well? What is going on?"

"The duke helped birth the colt. She was having trouble. We had to help her."

"But it is fine, the colt is well?"

"Big and strong. He was already nursing."

"Did she do well with him? This is her first time…"

"Yes, she knew what to do. A good mare."

"And how did his grace do?"

"Well…he did well."

"Good. I wonder what he will name it."

She shrugged. "I am tired, *Aitatxo*. Do you mind if I lay down for a bit?"

His eyebrows shot up, but he shrugged. She pushed past him to go up the stairs and sit on her bed. Her mind kept replaying the kiss over and over. She screwed her eyes shut as though that would keep the images from her mind. Sarah hugged herself, then lay down on the bed to stare blankly at the little dressing table.

There was a knock on the door, and she called out, "Come in."

Her father shuffled in with his cane. He sat heavily in the chair and looked at her with sad eyes. "Sarah, what happened?"

Tears sprang to her eyes and she dashed them away angrily. "Nothing, *Aitatxo*."

"Something, *Potxola*. You have never come in from a birth without checking the sex of the foal."

She sniffed. "The duke kissed me, *Aitatxo*." She waited for the outburst she knew was coming, but instead her father simply looked at her with sorrow.

"I must send you away, *Potxola*. And it will break my heart."

Her eyes widened and she swallowed. "*Aitatxo*, it will not happen again. I swear I did nothing to cause it."

"Hush, little one. I know. But he is a man, and you are a beautiful girl. And…I have kept a secret from you."

"What? What secret?"

He sighed and rose. She followed him to his own room where he went to his bookcase and removed an old book with a tattered cover. A paper extended beyond the margins of the pages. He pulled it free and handed her the letter. It was old, its edges roughened and corners dog-eared. Frowning, she opened it up and read.

Dear Sir,

I cannot call you by name for I do not know it, and that fact shames me. Years ago you stole my daughter away, only to lose her yourself. Perhaps I have grown old and soft, but I no longer feel the anger...only the sorrow for the loss of my child.

But, she gave you a daughter. I know this for she wrote to me once after the birth to tell me of the little Sarah. It occurs to me that this little Sarah must be almost a woman now, and that perhaps you might accept my help with her.

I am lonely. My wife is dead these many years, and my son recently died. I would ask that you share my daughter's child with me. I can promise to clothe her and show her the life her mother gave up for you. I will be honest, it is my hope she will fall in love with me and my home and stay with me. But I will not force her. Only let her choose.

me and stay with me. But I will not force her. Only let her choose.

Yours sincerely,

Edmund, Earl of Wrottlesby, Berkshire

She folded the letter and handed it back. "*Aitatxo,* is it true? I have a grandfather?"

"Yes, my little one. I received this four years ago,

and did not write him back. I was angry. I will admit it. Who was this man to steal my daughter from me? And then the accident, and I did not think I could spare you. But now, things have changed, and I think it is time you went to meet this earl, your grandfather."

"No, *Aitatxo*, don't send me away! Who will train the horses?"

"Henry shows promise. At least he will do what I tell him. He deserves a chance, just as you deserve a chance to be a fine lady."

A sob wracked her chest and she reached out for his arms. "Please, *Aitatxo*, no!"

He patted her back and said with a cracked voice. "And yet, I think you must go. It is time, my dear, to meet your mother's family." He followed her back to her room where she perched on the edge of the bed.

Then he left her and closed the door, while she curled on her side and cried.

Outside, the storm broke. Rain lashed the window and beat on the roof. Sarah lay on her bed and cried. But her tears did not last long, and soon she was up, looking through her things for what she would need to take with her.

Emma washed her dresses and helped pack an old trunk they found in the attic. When the rain cleared, Arnas ordered the cart readied with Bard, and Sarah climbed onto the box seat while her trunk was placed in the back. Emma's sister had gotten an old *pelisse* that was only a little too large for Sarah, and a straw bonnet for her to wear. She felt silly wearing them, but Emma impressed upon her the importance of doing so. Then, after a tearful goodbye, she hunkered against the cold on the box seat and watched them as she was pulled away.

As the cart passed the manor house, she stared up at its rambling wings with mixed emotions. The distance of a few days had allowed her to determine that while surprised, she had enjoyed her first kiss. But she also knew that she could not bear to see him again. She tore her gaze away and looked at the road ahead.

Berkshire lay nearly one hundred miles to the west. She would be changing to the post in the little city of Wexley. Then, it would take a good three days to get to Wrottlesby. Her father had sent a letter on ahead, and she carried her mother's jewels, such as they were, by way of introduction. She tried not to think beyond the next stage in her journey.

Sarah had rarely seen the city, and though it was small by London standards, in her eyes it seemed large and chaotic. The coach was huge compared to the Tensington carriage, and she had to fight for a spot inside. Once there, she had to hold her carryall in her lap and squeeze up to one side as a large lady took up much of the space on the seat. It did not take long at all for the trunks and boxes to be loaded and secured, and then the coach started forward with a lurch.

Sarah stared out the window at the countryside going by. The large lady to her right fell asleep and snored loudly in her ear and the little boy across the way kept kicking her legs. And always was the fear of the unknown which hovered over her.

Three days later, they pulled to a stop at an inn. Sarah climbed out, stiff and sore from days on the road. She found where her trunk had been deposited on the ground beside the inn. People went in all directions, crossing the street, going into the inn, disappearing through distant doors until she was all alone. Not knowing what to do, she sat down on her trunk and waited, clutching the thin *pelisse* around her and wishing for the overcoat she was used to wearing.

She dug out the letter her father had given her from the earl and read the direction beneath his name once again. Shadows spread across the street and lamps began to light windows up and down the street, but still there was no indication as to what she should do. Night fell, and with it, the temperature. She reached into the carryall, yanked out the small blanket Emma had packed for her, and pulled it around her shoulders. The straw bonnet was not much protection from the cold and she shivered a little.

From up the street came the sound of horses' hooves. A black carriage approached, pulled by two gray horses in perfect step. The carriage stopped before her and a groom hopped down to open the door.

An old man peered out, staring at her for some moments. She held out the letter.

"Please, sir, are you the Earl of Wrottlesby?"

The old man's face split and he chuckled. "Me? No. But I work for him. Are you Sarah Mondragón?"

"Yes, sir."

"Well come along, child. George will get your trunk."

She stood and the trunk was whisked out from underneath her. George grunted.

"Don't weigh nothin' it don't. What you got in here—one dress and a feather pillow?"

"Two dresses."

George grinned as he loaded her box onto the carriage. Then he handed her into the carriage and she made sure to sit across from the old gentleman.

"I am Speers, his lordship's secretary. I was his batman in the war, and now here I am with him still."

She tried to smile, but didn't quite and he cocked his head to one side.

"I suppose this is a big change for you. Well, well! Just you wait until we get you to Wrottlesby. Not so big as Withcombe, but comfortable for all that."

"Yes, sir."

"You have a look of your mother about you."

"You knew my mother?"

"Oh yes. She played many a prank on me as a child. Change your hair from black to gold and I daresay you'd easily be taken for her."

"I didn't know I looked like her."

"There's a painting in the gallery you can look at and judge for yourself. Ah." He pointed out the window to the large manor house. "Here we are."

"Will I see the earl tonight?"

"You mean your grandfather?" His eyebrows were up, but he smiled. "I shouldn't think so tonight, no. He is not in the best of health. But a warm supper, a hot bath, and a good night's sleep and you shall meet him in the morning, no doubt."

The carriage stopped and he motioned for her to get out as George stepped forward to help her down. She stared up at the rambling house that looked as though it had been cobbled together from several different houses. The door opened and a flood of warm air engulfed her. She moved instinctively toward it and stood in the foyer. The butler took her blanket and waited while she unbuttoned the *pelisse* to hand over as well. She felt a little ashamed of her plain blue dress and worn boots showing underneath.

Mr. Speers came in and ushered her toward an arched entrance to a room with a large fire blazing in the fireplace. She stared at the dark wainscot, the elaborate ceilings, and the plush looking furniture interspersed with inlaid cabinets and side tables. Candles burned everywhere and she hesitated to sit, but Speers waved her to a chair by the fire.

A footman brought in a tray with a teapot and a plate with a silver cover over it. The tray was set to one side and the boy stepped back as though waiting. Sarah looked up at him and then reached over to pour herself a cup of tea. As soon as she did so, the footman lifted the silver cover to reveal a cold supper of ham slices and a jelly.

While Sarah ate, there was a commotion in the hallway and she heard Speer's voice protesting. But the bustle grew closer and she looked up to see two figures entering the room. Both of them were elderly, a man and woman who looked remarkably alike.

"Oh! Edmund! She is the spitting image of Catherine!" the older woman cried.

"Her hair is her father's though, I'll bet. Here, girl, stand up and let's look at you."

"Edmund! Let her finish eating! Poor thing has been riding the post for days."

Sarah swallowed and pushed the tray aside, then stood, trying to hide her boots from sight. The keen gaze of Edmund, Earl of Wrottlesby, raked over her. He and the lady exchanged a glance. The woman smiled and sat beside her on the settee.

"I am Lady Genevieve Touillart, your great-aunt. This is Edmund, your grandfather."

"I am pleased to meet you both." She swallowed her nerves.

"Well, my dear, I hope you don't mind but I took it upon myself to engage a lady's maid for you. You will find her poorly trained, but I thought it might be nice for you both to learn together." She motioned to Speers, who stood beside the archway. "Ring for Elsie Brown, Speers."

Moments later, a girl with a rather thick waist appeared and bobbed a curtsey. Genevieve waved her over and the girl looked Sarah up and down, then curtseyed again.

"Miss Sarah Mondragón, your lady's maid Elsie Brown. Elsie, I thought we would start with a bath, and I have had some articles of clothing—shifts and nightdress, and dressing gown as well, placed in her room. I've put her in the Lavender Room. Go on, you know what to do."

Elsie bobbed another curtsey and scuttled off.

"Come, Genevieve. Let her get settled in. We will have all day tomorrow to play with our new toy." The earl leaned forward from his seat and took Sarah's hands in his own withered ones. "I hope you alleviate some of the shame brought on this house by your mother."

Lady Genevieve tapped her grandfather with the back of her hand. They walked from the room, leaning on each other. Her heart pattered a bit, fighting the surge of sorrow.

Speers cleared his throat. "I will show you to your room, miss."

The staircase went to a landing, then branched into two, each going to an opposite side. Paintings from centuries past littered the walls, barely visible in the gloom from her single candle. Speers did not seem to need a light to guide him through the dark halls. He stopped before a room and opened the door for her.

Several candles shone about the chamber, and a large tub stood in front of the little fire. Elsie was just finishing emptying a steaming can of water into the tub. She set it down and looked up.

"Bath's ready, miss."

"I'll leave you." Speers backed out and shut the door after him.

Sarah bit her lip and stared at the tub, then at Elsie who gestured to the water.

"I'd hurry, miss, before it gets cold."

Sarah set her carryall down and unbuttoned her drop-front gown. It fell into a heap around her. She struggled to free her feet until Elsie undid the laces of her boots and helped her take them off. With a self-conscious glance at Sarah, she undid the laces of her corset, then looked away as Sarah pulled her shift off and sank into the warm water of the tub.

She nearly groaned with pleasure. After fighting the cold in the carriage for days, to be suddenly surrounded by warmth was bliss. Elsie seemed to think that she should wash Sarah, but she took the sponge from her and washed herself. Elsie helped towel her dry, then lowered a fluffy confection of linen and lace over her head.

"What is this?"

"A nightgown, miss. You sleeps in it."

Sarah fingered the edge of the lace around the bodice, then stepped into the dressing gown Elsie held ready. She gazed around the room and sat in a chair next to a large dressing table. Elsie had already unpacked her meager set of brushes and toiletries. Her other two dresses hung in the wardrobe. Elsie wheeled the tub out and returned to pick up all of Sarah's castoff clothing.

"I'll be back with the bed warmer, miss."

"Oh, there's no need…"

"Lady Touillart will skin me alive if I don't." Then she was gone, leaving Sarah alone in the large room.

She was suddenly aware that her feet were cold, so she went to the fire, standing as close as she dared to it. The floor there was warm, and she let her toes soak it up before sitting back down. Elsie returned after a while, carrying a bed warmer. She held it in the fire for a few minutes, then slipped it under the covers of the bed. Sarah watched, intrigued.

When Elsie was done, she gestured to the bed. "It's ready for you, miss."

She removed the dressing gown, which Elsie stepped forward to take from her. Her toes recoiling from the cold floor, Sarah stepped over to the side of the bed and climbed in. As her legs slid down between the sheets, she felt only warmth instead of the shock of cold she was used to when climbing into bed.

What was her father doing just now? Rubbing his leg with liniment most likely and fondling Zigor's ears.

And the duke? What did he do at night? Perhaps he was kissing the woman he had visiting with him. Her mind envisioned the scenario and her gut clenched at the thought. Tears squeezed out, and she wondered what this pain was. Homesickness, yes, but there was something else when she thought of the duke.

A piercing stab that never seemed to go away…

Chapter Nine

William stared out at the rain. Short of storming down to the stables under a leaking umbrella, he was trapped in the mansion. Down there, lost in the rain, was a girl he felt unaccountably attracted to, and he wanted to see her.

He made his way to the parlor where Maggie sat with her round little chaperone. Mildred hunched over her embroidering, while Maggie stood at the window. She sighed when she caught sight of him.

"Rain. Whatever shall we do?"

"Endure it, I guess."

"Have you any abandoned wings where we could adventure like in some horrid gothic novel?"

"No such luck, I'm afraid."

She sighed again, for emphasis, and William's nerves rattled.. What was he to do? She had come to him...and he was starting to wonder why.

"Why are you here, Maggie?"

"Don't you remember? You invited me when we were at the Kents' house party some months ago. 'Maggie, my dear' you said. 'You must come see my horses.' So here I am, and have yet to see the creatures."

"We'll fix that once the rain stops. I have a new foal born. I even helped bring it into the world."

"Sounds disagreeable."

"No, it was actually quite splendid."

"I never took you for a 'hands-on' type."

"Nor did I. But there, I would be happy to do it again." All of it.

"Well not with all this rain, I wager."

"You could finish the altar cloth you started," Mildred said calmly, never lifting her gaze from the bit of cloth held close to her face.

Maggie turned a disdainful expression toward her cousin, then looked away. She leaned her head back against the chair and sighed. William sat nearby.

"We can take a ramble over Withcombe. No haunted galleries or wings that I know of, but some respectable tapestries and paintings."

She smiled at him. "That would be lovely. Perhaps after luncheon."

He picked up a book to give him an excuse to be quiet. His mind was full of Sarah—how to see her again, what to say…he felt he could not rest until he was near her once more.

But then what? Could he actually court the daughter of the horsemaster—no, his practicing horsemaster. Or would it be horsemistress? He imagined Sarah at a ball, wearing her little white dress with the old sash…He gave a small shake of his head. What was he saying? He could no more introduce her into society than fly.

What to do?

He stared out the window. Rivulets of water chased their way down the panes, distorting the view. Somewhere out there she was working with the horses, helping with another birth perhaps, supervising the grooms. He realized he wasn't sure what she did all day, only that she had been busy most times he'd seen her.

Must he let her go to another man and share his life? A knot of rage caught his breath and he let it go, slowly, fighting for control. He knew the answer. No matter what, he would find a way to make her his.

The afternoon came, and he found himself leading Maggie and Mildred around the manor. The housekeeper accompanied them, having much more insight into the furnishings and paintings than William.

"But surely," Maggie said, "You grew up here."

"I was away at school much of the time. When I was home, I was uninterested in the history of Withcombe or the horses. Now that I have had my own estate to run, I feel differently about these things."

"Yes, you have shown great interest in the horses."

"I must understand the business so I can make good decisions about the future of Withcombe's horses."

Mrs. Hinckley led them first to the gallery where she went through many of the paintings. She paused at one and began a long story about a cousin to the Tensingtons and a scandal that rocked the two families and caused a rift. There was mention of horses, but his mind drifted as he thought of Sarah's flashing eyes and quick hands.

Hinckley took them over most of the house, very thoroughly presenting every potential point of interest, and many that were of little interest. William, though, found himself growing more attached to the old estate, and beginning to understand his father a little more.

By the time they finished, they needed to hurry to dress for supper and William's valet tied his cravat with a set expression.

"That's enough, Larkin," William said good-naturedly as he turned to head down the hall to the staircase that led to the dining room.

It was empty, save for a footman. He went to his place and stood, waiting for his guests to arrive. Mildred came first, her dress unfashionable and her jewelry minimal. He was about to sit when Maggie swept in.

Her dress was a peacock silk with a gauzy overskirt and train. She wore brilliant opals set in gold at her throat and ears, and a small tiara. Her eyes were alight with the knowledge that she looked stunning.

"My dears, sorry if I am a teensy bit late. This dress put up quite a struggle!"

"The final effect is worth it!" said Mildred.

Maggie smiled stiffly, but shot a look toward William as though she would have liked a response from him. He simply nodded to her, however, and the first course was brought in.

Maggie and Mildred chattered for some time, until Maggie paused and leaned forward toward William. "Tensington!"

"Eh? What?"

"I said, what shall we do tomorrow?"

He sighed. "We are having a ball in a few days. Must we do something tomorrow?"

"You have been most distracted and inattentive today. What is wrong?"

"Nothing. The rain, I suppose…"

"Nonsense. There's something else I wager."

"I don't know what you are talking about."

With her head tilted birdlike to the side, she

considered him. "Humph. I shall winkle it out of you in time."

His brow creased as a spark of irritation rose. He stabbed a bite of squab and raised it to his mouth. Reaching for his glass of wine, he noted it was empty and signaled for it to be refilled. He wondered what Sarah was doing now…

"And I said to her, Clara, you are going to have to marry someone. It might as well be Lord Swingledon," Maggie said in between bites.

"Oh, and they had such a lovely wedding," Mildred purred.

"Yes, I suppose it was. The wedding breakfast was certainly good. And, I know for a fact that he agreed to purchase a townhome for her so she would not have to go to the country so often."

"Why would that be necessary?" William asked.

"Oh, your grace, surely you wouldn't want to spend all your time in the country! Really, I'm sure you enjoy your time in London."

It was no good. William put down his fork and tossed his napkin down as well. He rose.

"If you'll excuse me, I am going down to the stables to check on the foals."

The two women looked blankly at him, their movements arrested in mid-air. He strode from the room and out into the foyer where the butler met him, and quickly sent a footman scrambling for the duke's overcoat. William shouldered into it and then stepped free of the manor to head down to the warm lights of the stable buildings.

He went first to the broodmares' stalls, peering over the door at the foal he had helped bring into the world. Pride surged through him as he looked at the sturdy colt walking about on long legs. The mare ambled over to him and stuck her head out the door. He stroked her smooth neck, and wished he had thought to bring a treat.

He looked into the other stalls, noting that more foals had been born. He headed for the cottage, lured by the gentle glow from candlelight within.

Barking began as soon as he rang the bell, and he heard the stump and slide of Arnas's advance. Why wasn't Sarah coming to spare her father the agonizing progress? Instead, the old horsemaster himself opened the door, pushing the dog back as he did so.

"Duke Tensington! How may I help you?"

"I wanted to discuss names for the foals with you and your daughter."

"You may discuss it with me. Sarah is not here."

Shock rooted William to the ground, his mouth opened but it took a moment to find his voice. "Where is she?"

Arnas looked aside. "She has gone to visit relatives."

"How long will she be gone?"

"I don't know. Some time, I am sure. Did you want to come in?"

"I…yes. Of course." He stepped into the narrow foyer, all thoughts in his head flown.

Arnas limped toward a small table and sat down. He reached behind him, pulled out a large ledger, and retrieved an inkstand and pen.

"So, names for the new foals. Two colts and a filly. The first is the one out of Poppy by Tunbridge Blue Burn." He paused and looked up at the duke.

"I think I will let your daughter name him."

Arnas's eyes widened slightly, but he went on to the next. "This is the little colt out of Gertie by Tunbridge Blue Burn."

"Withcombe...Fire?"

"Can I suggest something like Withcombe Fire and Ice, or Fiery Heritage, or such like?"

"Fire and Ice, then."

Arnas wrote and blotted the ink. "The last is a filly born out of Gwendolyn by Alston Straight Arrow. He's a thoroughbred. He sired our own Hallington's Hopeful Promise."

"A filly, you say?"

"Yes."

"Then, how about Withcombe Bonny?"

Arnas wrote.. "How else may I help you, your grace?"

"With Sarah gone, who is taking over training?"

"Henry Tench. He has some promise. I am watching him closely."

"Good. Good. Well, I think that is all." He stood, feeling foolish and wanting to ask where, specifically, Sarah had gone but not knowing how. Instead he nodded and headed out the door.

The rain had eased off, making the umbrella unnecessary. He headed up the slight rise toward the manor house, windows alight with ghostly flickering from candles. Sarah, gone? To relatives? Which relatives? Arnas was Basque. Surely they hadn't sent her to Spain...What of her mother? He knew nothing about her, only that there was some scandal involved. Who would know?

William made it to the house to find that Maggie

and Mildred had retired to the sitting room. He joined them, momentarily contrite for abandoning them. Maggie looked up from the pianoforte with an arch expression.

"Ah! Done conspiring with your little horse girl?"

"What? No! She is long gone. I had to talk to her father about the foals. Pedigrees and names and such."

She fingered a bar. "Sounds tedious."

He said nothing, simply sat and picked up a book. He stared through it, but turned a page now and then to give the illusion he was reading.

But William could not stop wondering where Sarah Mondragón had gone.

Chapter Ten

Sarah woke in the dark hours of the morning, aware of someone in her room. Easing open her eyes, she stared through the gloom to see a figure bent over the fire.

"Who are you and what are you doing here?" she whispered.

The figure jumped and turned around, hand to chest. "Oh, miss, you scared me! It's only me, Elsie, stoking your fire."

"Why?"

"So your room will warm for you." She frowned and added, "Why are you awake already? It's still dark out."

Sarah pushed herself up from the bed and rubbed a stiff spot in her neck. "I'm used to getting up to take care of the horses."

"Nothing like that for you to do here."

"What will I do?"

"That's a question for 'is lord and ladyship." She frowned and glanced around. "I did hear mention of a dancing master."

Sarah's face twisted in disgust. A wave of homesickness came over her, longing for a place where she had a purpose. How was Blue? Was he in a pasture yet? Had any more of the mares foaled? How were Poppy and her little colt doing? How were *Aitatxo* and

Emma and all the stable lads? If only she knew…

"Miss? Did you hear me? I was askin' if you wanted to go down to breakfast, or have me bring it to you?"

"Oh, I will go down, Elsie."

"Which dress will you wear?"

"The white one, I guess. I can do it by myself, if you have something else to be doing."

"If you don't mind, I'll help you, seeing as how you're my job."

Sarah paused for a moment. "Oh. I'm not so sure about this."

"Oh, please, miss. If you send me away they'll stick me back with the maids."

"I just…I'm not used to all this attention."

"Well, miss, this is how it is. I like my work with you."

"Oh…I…well then, all right."

Elsie's round face collapsed in relief. "Here, let's get you into your shift and stays."

So Sarah let Elsie lift off her night gown and drop her shift over her head. After the corset was laced, Sarah slipped on her only petticoat. Then Elsie set her gown over her head and straightened it all the way down. She was fastened up, and Elsie stepped back to look at her.

"I suspect Lady Touillart will be ordering you all new things. For now, wear this pair of slippers. I cleaned them up as best I could."

"Right. Now may I go eat?"

"Let's fix your hair. Sit, please."

Elsie proceeded to brush her hair out and twist it into an elaborate bun. The tendrils that escaped were curled and set.

"There, now you may go. Do you need me to show you the way?"

"Yes, actually. If you don't mind."

"Not at all. Come with me."

They set out into the long dark hallway with its paintings and candelabras. Elsie led her to the stairs, then pointed to a pair of doors thrown open on the first floor.

"That's the breakfast room. You serve yourself."

"Okay. I can handle that!" She set off down the carved wooden staircase and turned into the breakfast room. She found it empty, but several warming trays of food were set up. She picked up a plate and scooped in a little of everything, then sat down to study her surroundings.

A footman came in with a salver containing a single letter. He set it down beside her and she reached slowly for it. Recognizing her father's handwriting, she quickly broke the seal to read,

My dearest daughter,

I hope this finds you well. We miss you already, but I know you are in a good place. You will want to know about the horses—well, what can I tell you? Blue is going out to pasture every day now that most of the brood mares are in foaling boxes. So far he seems to like it. He is ready to come in each night, however, and get his warm mash!

Poppy and her baby do well; he is growing fast. It has been raining since you left so we have not seen his grace or I would have insisted on a name for him. We have had two more born since you went away—one colt and one filly. Both are well and strong.

Hope was a little unmanageable today. He is restless with all this rain. I had a boy walk him out in the damp anyway and he pranced away while getting wet. We had to dry him and blanket him when he was done. And I may have ordered him a warm mash as well.

Emma and I are well, but we miss you. I did not know how much I depended upon you until you were gone. But do whatever your grandfather tells you to do. He wants to teach you to be a lady, and that can't hurt you. Please write me so I know you are safe and well.

d well.

Your loving Aitatxo

Tears sprang to her eyes and with a sniffle she wiped them away. A throat cleared and she looked up to see her grandfather standing there.

"Your lordship…"

"Grandfather will do."

She swallowed against the pressure in her throat. "Grandfather, then."

He helped himself to a plate and came to sit across from her. He nodded at the letter in her hand and said, "Good news, I hope."

She nodded. "Yes, he writes to tell me all are well—even the new foals."

"Ah, that's right. The horses. I take it you share your father's passion for them."

"Yes, I do."

"Then we must certainly do something about that. I have a horse that may suit you. We shall have to get you a riding habit."

"You mean…to ride sidesaddle? I tried it a few times, but I don't like it."

His white eyebrows rose high in his pink face. "Indeed. Well, perhaps we can help you learn to like it better. There are certain rules for behavior, and ladies must ride sidesaddle."

She swallowed, eyes wide.

"My sister will be working with you to improve your wardrobe, and later today I thought we would take a carriage tour of the estate."

"Oh yes, please!"

"You would like that, then?"

"I would, very much."

He smiled slightly. The tips of his mustache moved and his eyes crinkled. It reminded her of her mother, somehow, and warmth rose within her. Heels clattered in the hall and looked up in time to see Lady Touillart drift into the room, with a floating shawl wafting from her arms and the most delicate chemisette Sarah had ever seen."

"Ah, there you are. Nice healthy appetite, excellent. I'm sure I won't have to remind you to get your daily exercise."

"I was just telling her I may have a horse for her."

"Oh, what luck. Saves us finding one. And, I dare say, I will have the *modiste* in today to take your measurements. What are your favorite colors?

Sarah thought for a moment. "You know the color of a clear sky just before it becomes night? That dark, dark blue with the hint of green underneath. And the golden brown you see in some horse's eyes when they are a light bay."

Her grandfather and great-aunt exchanged a glance.

"Y-y-yes. I see. I think we can find a way to bring those colors into your wardrobe. Have you finished your breakfast?"

"Yes, ma'am."

"Come along, then. The *modiste* will be here soon."

Sarah rose and bobbed a quick curtsey to her grandfather before following her great-aunt out into one of the sitting rooms. A small piano sat in it and Sarah sat on the little bench and touched a few keys. She smiled, looking up at Genevieve.

"I always wanted to learn the piano."

The older woman smiled. "It is a useful skill. Perhaps we can find a music master to teach you. Though you are a little old to begin. Your mother had great talent."

"I know she missed it, and *Aitatxo* was trying to find her a small piano when she died."

"*Aitatxo*?"

"It's my father's language. It means daddy."

"Why did he not get it for you, then?"

She shrugged. "I was always busy with the horses, so I would not have had time, and there was no one to teach me." She rose and wandered around the room, reaching out to touch the various objects.

The butler arrived with a tall woman in tow. She wore a pair of spectacles and started when she caught sight of Sarah.

"Lady Touillart, is this the person you spoke of?"

"Yes, Miss Vanwelder. She needs everything—shifts, petticoats, a new corset, and dresses! She'll need at least three afternoon dresses, and a couple of evening gowns to start with. Oh, and a *pelisse*. She can use her current dresses as morning dresses until you can make those also. Just so you can organize the process. Shoes, too, if you can handle it?"

"I can take measurements with a tracing and give them to old Groebel. He can make her some nice, laced boots and some slippers."

"I don't need to emphasize the urgency of this."

"No, my lady. I will have my whole staff work on this. We'll get it done."

As they were talking, Miss Vanwelder used a tape measure on Sarah, silently indicating for her to turn, lift her arms, etc. All the while she jotted in a small book. Finally she finished with Sarah and stood, making a few more notes, then nodded. "All right, I think I've got it. Any colors in particular?"

Genevieve looked at Sarah and beckoned her close. She held out a folded piece of paper and said, "Are these the colors you were talking about?"

Spread on the paper were swirls of different colors, all shades of what Sarah had tried to describe. She smiled and nodded.

"How did you make this?"

"Watercolors, my dear." Genevieve handed the paper to Miss Vanwelder. "If you could use this as a palette."

Her bespectacled eyes peered down at the colors, and she nodded curtly. "I believe I have some materials in stock. All right, I will get busy on this." She picked up her bag and strode away, leaving Sarah alone with Genevieve.

"That is going to cost a lot…"

Genevieve held up a hand. "Hush. We will not discuss it. I am enjoying myself thoroughly."

Sarah's smile warred with emotions that threatened to overwhelm her excitement over the clothes, homesickness, and a strange yearning to see the duke again. She touched her lips lightly with her fingers, then rubbed her hands which had cooled in the cold air of the parlor.

Genevieve called a servant and ordered more coal for the fire and tea to be brought in. "There," she said, "We will have some refreshment before Edmund whisks us off on a carriage ride. He probably can't wait to show off his new *barouche*." Genevieve poured out, her lined hand shaking a little as she handed Sarah her cup. "Now, what brings you to Wrottlesby?"

Sarah's gaze shot up. "What do you mean? His lordship wrote to my father…"

"Yes, but that was years ago. What happened to bring you here now?"

Sarah stared at the milk swirling in her tea. Carefully setting the spoon down, she said, "Poppy, my favorite mare, was in trouble foaling. His grace came in to help me and we pulled the foal free together. Then…he kissed me."

"Ah…"

"Father thought it best that I get away."

"Yes, I can see why. You are safe here."

Sarah smiled a little, looking at the elderly woman with real gratitude. "Yes, ma'am. I know. Thank you."

"Was the little foal all right?"

"Oh yes, he's a strong little thing. He was up and drinking from his mother in no time. And she was such a good mother, though he was her first. I wonder what the duke will name him…"

"What would you name him if you could?"

Sarah's smile widened. "Withcombe's Flight of Fancy."

Genevieve's eyebrows shot up. "Indeed! Impressive name."

"Yes, but I shan't get the chance. He is named by now."

The earl wandered in and came to sit on the elegant, but worn, couch. "Ah, my dears. And are you ready for our adventure? I have had the kitchen pack us a picnic."

"Oh, what fun. Are they bringing a table and chairs as well?"

"Yes. They are setting up by the old abbey. Don't worry, we won't be sitting on the ground."

"Well, I am pleased to hear it." She set her empty cup down in the saucer and pushed stiffly to her feet.

Sarah joined them, and together they went out the front door where a shining *barouche* pulled by a pair of bays stood.

"Now, missy, take a look at those horses. What do you think?"

Sarah studied them, then turned to the earl with wide eyes. "Are they Withcombe Bays?"

"Indeed they are, though I am about ready to retire the pair of them. I bought them through a friend, many years ago, to have something of my daughter at hand."

They started off, and Sarah watched with interest as the countryside passed by. They passed farms, and the earl talked knowledgably about the crops and the tenants who worked them. Sarah was interested to see cows in one field, and to hear that the farm made its own cheese, which was served in the Wrottlesby kitchen.

"Oh, please, sir! Can I try it some time?"

"You will try it at luncheon, today. I made sure

they packed some for us."

By the time they reached the old abbey, Sarah was hot and hungry. The abbey rose like a skeleton from the grassy hill, great and partial arches reaching upward against the blue of the sky. Sarah could not stop staring at them.

The table had been set up in the shade, for which everyone was relieved after riding in the bright sunshine all morning. A footman filled a plate for Sarah and set it before her, but she watched her aunt and grandfather to see how they ate. With their fork, apparently, held just so…

Sarah tried to emulate them, and if she was a little clumsy at first, they did not seem to notice. Though her aunt did comment on her posture.

"Now dear, sit up straight and don't slouch."

"Yes, Aunt"

"Edmund, this has been delightful, but I am tired."

"Yes, sister, let's get you home."

The footman helped them all into the *barouche.*, Sarah snagged an extra piece of the cheese from the table before being helped up.

The ride home was quiet, and Sarah's mind wandered as she watched the farms roll by. The Withcombe Bays pulled the carriage securely and in perfect time and rhythm. It only intensified the sense of homesickness she felt. A restless energy coursed through her, and she wanted badly to be doing something.

"What are you thinking, Sarah?"

"That I am not used to leisure. I have worked my whole life and feel the need to be doing something."

"Perhaps tomorrow I can get a horsemaster in to

teach you sidesaddle. Then you can start riding."

"Oh, I would like to see the horses!"

He chuckled. "Well then, let me see what I can do."

Chapter Eleven

William stared through the fire, waiting for the dinner gong. He tugged at his cravat. Larkin had tied it a little snug this evening. The ladies were not down yet, but they would be. And then would begin the inane comments and attempts at social intercourse. None of it solving the riddle of where was Sarah Mondragón?

But the ball was only one day away, and then they would be leaving. He sighed in anticipation of the event. He was ready to have his house to himself so he could brood in peace.

Voices floated down from the staircase, and he went out to meet the ladies. Maggie took his arm and all but pulled him along to the dining room, while Mildred trailed behind. He made sure that they were seated before taking his own chair at the head of the table.

It still felt strange to him to be in a position of authority in his father's house. Slowly, though, he was becoming used to the ways of the manor and even finding he preferred it to Marwinne in many ways. Thinking of Marwinne reminded him that his mother would be coming in a couple of weeks, and that he would have to remind the staff to get her suite ready.

"What shall we do this evening?" Maggie asked.

"Backgammon? Chess?" William said.

"Music!" Mildred sighed.

Maggie smiled. "Certainly I will be happy to play."

William tried to copy her smile. "That will be lovely."

"I am so looking forward to the ball tomorrow night."

"Oh! I can't wait to see all the couples dancing and hear the quartet playing," Mildred said.

"It's a septet," William said.

"Oh, my!" Mildred nearly dropped her spoon.

They worked their way through the courses and then into the parlor where the pianoforte stood. Maggie sat down, taking some time to arrange her skirt. The she started on a slow waltz that floated through the room.

William listened with half an ear as he stared into the fire, wondering yet again how he would find Sarah. He was of a mind to charge down to the stables and demand to know where she was, but knew he would look like a fool if he did.

Perhaps he no longer cared.

Maggie played for a while, then stretched elaborately and declared, "I am tired tonight. I think I will go to bed to be refreshed for tomorrow."

"Oh, yes, dear. That would be best. I will join you once I finish this flower. Mildred peered close to her embroidery and slipped her needle into a spot.

"Perhaps I will find a groom to fall in love with!" Her tinkling laughter died away as she disappeared up the staircase.

William rose and bowed as Maggie swept out. He sat back slowly, thinking. His mind went to the story Mrs. Hinckley had told them and he wondered if it was related in any way to Sarah. Except her father wasn't a groom...or had he been?

He rang the bell and asked for the housekeeper to

be called. It took several minutes, but then she stood before him, forbidding in all black.

"Mrs. Hinckley. Do you remember the tour you gave the marchioness and myself?"

She inclined her head.

"You told a story about a family connected to Withcombe and a tragic love story. Can you repeat that?"

"Certainly. The Earl of Wrottlesby's girl and a groom from our stables. She was a great rider, so they met often at the stables. They ran off one night, and the earl disowned her flat and swore never to step foot on Withcombe again."

"What happened to the girl…and the groom?"

"They lived here. She died some years ago, but he is the horsemaster of the stables. I believe they had a…"

"Daughter. Her name is Sarah."

"Yes, that sounds about right. Is that all?"

"Yes, Hinckley. Thank you."

Wrottlesby! He had a place, now to find out where it was. So had the old earl relented and invited her? Had she simply shown up there? It did not matter, so long as he could find the place.

But first, he had a ball to get through.

It rained for the first part of the next day, but the sun peeked out briefly and helped dry the grass. The ballroom had been cleared, and the supper tables arranged in an adjoining room. He did not see Maggie or Mildred, and assumed they were sleeping late or keeping to their rooms in preparation for the evening.

Larkin had gotten out his midnight blue jacket and black trousers. They were a relatively new fashion, and he had found he preferred them over breeches. His cravat was tied and his shoes slipped on, and it was time to go downstairs.

He stood in the foyer, waiting for the first guests to arrive. He could not remember the guest list, indeed he had left it mostly to Hinckley who knew the local families. He listened to the guests' names announced and greeted each with a smile. Time dropped seconds one by one into the background as family after family arrived and had to be welcomed.

It seemed as though the evening must be halfway over by the time the last straggling guests were in and he could join the throng in the ball room. He looked around for Maggie, thinking she would be the best young lady to open the ball with. He found her at the far end of the ball room, dressed in peacock blue. He asked her quickly to dance, and she smiled brilliantly in response and took his arm.

The band played the opening bars of the first song, The Polonaise "Grand" March, and he led her to the top of the room. They were joined by other couples and the dance began.

He prided himself on his dancing ability, and Maggie's eyes lit up with pleasurable surprise by the time they reached the second turn. He swung her to the left, they traded partners and then were back and promenading down the center. Heads turned their way and he knew he should be enjoying himself immensely.

Only, he wasn't.

His mind kept going back to a shadowed stall and a mare in distress. A courageous girl at his side as they pulled a foal into the world and helped it to take its first breaths. He had felt alive in that moment, more so than in this one where he was simply showing off.

They turned, and he fumbled the step.

Maggie's eyes flew wide and her smile vanished. They recovered quickly, but her smile was slow to return. The dance ended with couples once again facing each other and he reached out to lead her from the floor.

"I must apologize for missing that step."

"Nonsense, I barely noticed."

"You are too kind." He led her to a seat and stood beside her for a moment, only to be approached by a young man dressed all in navy blue. William recognized him enough to know they had been introduced, but could not recall his name.

"Lord Winchell, of Hamden Downs. I also raise horses."

"Oh, indeed. I have only just inherited Withcombe, but I am figuring it all out."

"Yes, it takes some doing. I was hoping I could have a glimpse of the famous Withcombe Bays."

"Certainly. Let us walk down now."

"You don't mind?"

"Not at all. What types of horses do you breed?"

"Thoroughbreds, but I just imported an Arabian stallion to infuse into the bloodline."

"I don't know much about either. I am still learning about our own horses. But what I can't answer, old Arnas can."

"Ah yes, Arnas Mondragón. I have heard of him."

"Have you?"

"I doubt there are many in the county who have not."

The changed out of their dancing shoes and set out down the narrow path. The butler provided them with a lamp and the two men followed the little track down the slope toward the lights in the cottage. They came around the entrance to the quadrangle and went to Blue's stall. William lifted the lantern and the light shone on Blue, standing in the far corner. His head popped up with the light, and he nickered before stepping toward them.

"Tunbridge Blue."

"Retired now, I hear. But what a record!"

"Indeed. One of his last foals was born not two weeks ago. Here, I'll show you. I was there for its birth."

"There is nothing like bringing a foal into the world."

"I would have to agree," William said.

He led the way past other stalls, with curious heads bobbing over the doors. He paused at Hallington's Hope and patted the reddish brown neck.

Lord Winchell did so as well and asked, "Who is this fine boy?"

"I can't remember his full name, but he is called Hope and he is the newest stallion to the herd."

"Hope for Withcombe Bays."

"Indeed."

They continued on and William led him to the broodmares' stalls, holding the lantern up over Poppy's door.

"This little lad doesn't have a name yet. I'm giving that honor to Mondragón's daughter. She has taught me what little I know. But he is one of the last of Blue's offspring."

They gazed upon the foal asleep next to its mother who lay curled around him. A sound came from behind them, a slide-stump with the clattering of a stick and the two men turned around to see the frowning face of Arnas Mondragón.

"Your grace! I saw lights and wondered who was wandering about."

"I'm sorry, Mondragón. Lord Winchell expressed an interest in the horses so we came down."

"Ah, Lord Winchell—of Hamden Downs. Lovely thoroughbreds! You have a new trainer there."

"Indeed! And a new stallion, like you. He is an Arabian."

"Smart, from what I hear! Is he difficult to work with?"

"Denning, my trainer, says he catches on quickly, it's just a question of whether or not he wishes to comply with commands."

Arnas chuckled, and William felt a little as though he didn't quite catch the joke. But the two men had moved on to discussing the issues with foaling and he noted that Arnas's forehead pinched in pain.

"Mondragón, you need to sit. Let's go to your house and continue this conversation."

Lord Winchell looked a little sheepish. "Your grace, I should probably get back to my wife, and you will be needed, I am sure."

"Ah, yes. The ball. I had quite forgotten."

Arnas chuckled again and said, "Horses will get in your blood, and you will never get them out."

The two peers walked Arnas back to his cottage, Lord Winchell asking questions as they went and Arnas answering them, his slight accent sounding even more foreign in the shadows cast by the lamp.

Together the two men walked up the rise to the

house, where they changed into their dancing shoes and rejoined the ball, to find that they had been absent for nearly two hours. William glanced around and heard his name called. Maggie strode toward him. A deep crease marred the otherwise perfect brow..

"Where have you been?" she demanded.

He frowned. "Lord Winchell and I went down to see the horses."

"Horses? This is a ball!"

"Yes, *my* ball."

"You do not simply walk out on a ball to go look at horses."

"Well, I just did. And I enjoyed myself. The dancing has gone along just fine without me."

Maggie's mouth fell open as he brushed past her to the refreshment table to chat with some of the mothers and chaperones clustered about while their charges danced in the next room.

He glanced in now and then, occasionally dancing with one of the wall flowers, something that made him think of Sarah even more. The hours spent down in the stables had made him feel close to her as nothing else had. He could not believe he had not asked after her…but then Lord Winchell and Mondragón had been thick in their discussion.

He would know soon enough about Sarah Mondragón.

Chapter Twelve

Gray skies blanketed the countryside, but Sarah did not care. Today she would be riding a horse, and her heart was alight.

The only shadow over her happiness was the riding habit she was forced to wear. It was a deep twilight blue. Her new corset felt stiff, and she was so blanketed by close-fitting layers that she felt almost claustrophobic. After spending most of her years in loose-fitting clothes and riding astride, today she was fitted out like a young lady, with her aunt and grandfather set to watch her ride. She saw the horse being led up the rise and straightened her posture.

The groom helped her up and she settled into the strange saddle, trying to remember the times she had ridden in her mother's. The center of gravity was different, and she would need to use the little crop to help communicate with the horse. She looked at her grandfather.

"Please, sir, what is his name?"

"Alsington's King Arthur. I call him Arthur."

"Arthur."

His ears swiveled back toward her. She adjusted the reins and squeezed with her leg and he walked in a circle. It was a little more awkward getting him to turn in a right-hand circle, however he did it and she breathed out a sigh of relief. She guided the horse in a large figure eight, then urged him into a trot. Coming up with the rise of the horse's step felt odd, but she managed it.

Genevieve remarked, "Very pretty. Can you canter him?"

Sarah urged Arthur and tapped with the crop. He lunged into a canter and she very nearly slipped off the right side. He faltered beneath her fumbling and stopped as she reseated herself.

"*Arraoia!*"

Edmund cleared his throat and said, "Language, my dear."

"It's just an old Basque word…"

"Words like that sound the same in any language. Please refrain from using them."

Sarah blew out a breath and tried the canter again. This time she adjusted her balance as they turned and she stayed neatly in place.

"Well done, my dear!"

"Thank you, Aunt."

She urged the horse a little faster and Arthur sped into a gallop across the field. Her soul sang with the burst of energy from the animal beneath her and she almost laughed out loud with delight.

Feeling the horse begin to tire, she pulled him into a gentle lope and turned to go back to where her grandfather and aunt sat watching. She breathed out a satisfied breath and grinned as she approached them.

"My dear! That was breathtaking!" Edmund said.

"It was! I like your horse!"

"He is yours, now. We shall have to have a hunt and show you off!"

"You mean, with dogs and such?"

"Hounds, dear. But yes."

"After the fox?"

"Yes."

"Do they kill the fox?"

Her grandfather cleared his throat and said, "Er…yes. That is the point. Foxes, you know, steal chickens and eggs and chicks. This is one way to keep their numbers down."

"I see." She reined Arthur around and trotted him in a broad circle, then cantered off toward the edge of the manor to ride around it..

What did the duke think of her being gone? Was he angry? Or perhaps he did not care…

She felt suddenly down, and Arthur seemed to sense it, for his steps became lethargic and he slowed. She rode past the gardens with their stone wall and finally reached the other side of the manor. As she came round the front, her aunt and grandfather waved to her and the earl stood as though waiting for her to return.

After riding up to him, she reached down to stroke the smooth neck of Arthur while her grandfather nodded in approval.

"Well, my dear, you have taken to that quite readily."

"Yes. This will be an excellent way for you to get exercise. That, and your dancing lessons."

Cold water washed over her soul. "Must I, Aunt?"

Genevieve looked at her through her gray lashes. "Yes, you must. It won't be as bad as you think. You may even enjoy it."

"Your mother quite liked dancing. It was one of her many accomplishments," the old earl said.

A frisson of irritation shot through Sarah. She was not her mother.

A groom stepped forward and held Arthur's bridle while Sarah slipped down. She walked a little stiffly to her aunt as Edmund spoke to the groom. Finally, he joined them and they went into the house together.

Sarah went upstairs to change out of her riding habit. Elsie met her and pulled out one of the new afternoon dresses. This was a golden brown with a slightly gathered bodice and van dyke points on the sleeves. Sarah loved it, and sighed with real happiness as it was lowered over her head and pulled into shape around her.

She watched in the mirror as it was fastened in back and the ribbons tied. The doorbell rang in the manor and she wondered who was visiting. She slipped on her newest little boots and went down the stairs to the parlor—only to find a pair of strangers there.

A woman with dark hair and an elaborate bonnet and *pelisse*, and a younger girl in lovely blue that matched her eyes were seated with her aunt. The earl was nowhere to be seen. She paused for a moment upon seeing them, then sat where her aunt indicated, near the younger lady.

"Mrs. Esterhay, Lavinia, this is my great-niece, Sarah Mondragón."

Both ladies bowed their heads and Sarah belatedly did the same. Her aunt spoke in low tones to Mrs. Esterhay and Sarah turned to Lavinia.

"Hello, do you live near here?"

"Yes, in West Redditch, the town down in the vale."

"Oh! I had wondered what that was called."

"Yes. I had heard you had come to stay, how do you like it?"

"I do. My riding habit finally arrived so I was able to ride out today and that was great fun."

Lavinia's eyes lit up. "Oh, do you like to ride? We must ride together sometime!"

"I should like that!"

They chatted for a time, Sarah questioning her closely about her horse when a little silence fell.

"Lavinia, dear, it is time to go." Mrs. Esterhay's voice was rather bland.

"Mama, Miss Mondragón likes to ride."

"That is excellent. You must ride together sometime."

Sarah stood as their guests readied themselves to leave. *Pelisses* were brought out and the pair helped into them, then they entered the waiting carriage and were gone.

Her aunt turned to her and said, "And now, piano!"

Sarah went to the pianoforte in the end of the room and sat on the polished seat. She worked hard, trying to remember her lessons and was pleased to see that it was all coming together for her. Her aunt tapped and nodded in time.

"Very good. You have your mother's touch already."

Her fingers stilled and she sat staring through the music. Her mother? What about her father? How was *Aitatxo*? She had not heard from him since that first letter. How were the horses? She missed it all—the smell of hay and horses, stable lads working in stalls, grooms grooming the horses. Training with her father barking commands. All of it. And she sat here dressed in her fine gown sitting at a glowing white piano in a glittering room—doing nothing terribly productive. Yet a part of her wished the duke could see her now. She wondered what he would think.

"Are you tired, Sarah?"

"What? Oh, no, ma'am. Just thinking."

"You looked very far away."

"I was." She started again, working through the simple music slowly. For nearly an hour she went over her lessons and the simple songs given her to practice, her aunt interjecting little pointers now and then. Finally, her aunt rang for tea. Sarah closed the instrument and came to sit with her.

"You did quite well with the Esterhay girl. We should probably have a supper and invite some families. Some of the girls will play and exhibit their talents, but you will not be expected to do so. It will just be a chance to introduce you into some sort of society."

The thought knifed through her. She swallowed a sudden shiver of nerves by taking a sip of tea. Genevieve passed her a plate of little sandwiches. She accepted one and ate it in little nibbles like she had seen her aunt do. A wave of homesickness swept over her and her hand with the sandwich fell slowly to her lap. Her aunt's fine silver eyebrows met in her lined forehead.

"What are you thinking, dear."

"Just…my father."

"Ah. Of course. He has been your world, has he not? It has been just you and your father for many years now."

"Yes, and he's so lame since his accident and he depends upon me. I'm worried for him."

"Suppose you were to marry, and go to live with your husband—what would your father do?"

"I…I don't know if I could do that to him…"

"And yet, surely he will expect you to do just that. One day…you are how old now? Nearly twenty. Many girls younger than you get married."

A sudden image of the duke's face as he bent to kiss her struck her and she barely stopped herself from gasping. If only it were possible to marry him…

She pushed the thought away. He would marry someone like the lady who had looked down her nose at her. The thought stabbed deep into her heart and she stared down at her hands. Marry somebody? Impossible, unless it were somehow the duke…

"I won't leave my father. He needs me."

"With you gone, who is helping him?"

She shook her head. "I don't know. Emma and Henry, I suppose."

"Who is Henry?"

"He is my father's assistant. Father says he has promise…and yet he sets me above him. I have been learning at his knee since I was a babe. Like him, I eat and breathe the horses. I understand them, and they understand me. Tell me, Aunt, what sort of man would have a woman like me?"

Genevieve's white head tilted like a bird's on her delicate neck. "Oh, my dear. Do not sell yourself so short."

****

The night of the supper and musicale arrived. The clear, sunny day faded into a starry night. Sarah's gaze met Elsie's in the mirror. She had arranged her hair in a coiled bun with curled tendrils with a pair of filigree combs her aunt had pressed upon her. Her dress was a deep twilight blue with a tantalizingly low neckline. She felt suddenly grown up and feminine, and wished the duke were going to be there to see her.

She reached into the boxes of jewelry that had belonged to her mother and pulled out the tiny pearls. Elsie fastened the latch on the pearls and stepped back.

Candles glowed and flickered as she descended the staircase to join her aunt and grandfather welcoming the guests. Sarah smiled when she saw Lavinia Esterhay and remarked on her dress.

"Oh, and yours is lovely too! That blue!"

Mrs. Esterhay gave her daughter a gentle shove. They left and were replaced by another family. Sarah was forced to smile for the strangers and shift her attention. She found herself confronted by a handsome young man who took her hand, with real delight in his eyes.

"Reginald Haustman, Sarah Mondragón," her aunt said.

Sarah's gaze followed him and then turned to the next in line. So it went until all the guests were accounted for and her grandfather led the way into the parlor where everyone sat or stood in light conversation. Sarah glanced over them, noting the Hanson family of three young ladies whose names escaped her. The spinster sisters and their young ward—a shy girl with mousy brown hair nicely arranged around her heart-shaped face. Her name was Olive, though Sarah could not recall her last name. Reginald and another young man, and of course the Esterhays.

Her great-aunt went to Olive and though Sarah

could not hear what was said, that girl shot a frightened glance at her mother before nodding shyly and going to the piano. The conversation in the room slowly died and all turned to the girl at the piano.

"Tell me, Miss Mondragón, will we have the pleasure of hearing you play?" Reginald whispered to her.

"No, it is not one of my accomplishments."

"I look forward to discovering your accomplishments!"

She hushed him and turned her attention to Olive who had begun. That she was nervous was evident in the hesitant chords and occasional misfingering. She grew bolder, however, and finished well to much applause. She was followed by one of the Hanson girls, each of whom played in sequence, then finally Lavinia.

Lavinia started timidly, but seemed to grow more confident as she went. Hers was by far the most complex of the arrangements, and the room burst into applause before the last note had died away. The room buzzed for a few more minutes in conversation before the gong rang and her grandfather rose to lead the company into the dining room.

Sarah felt a moment of pride when she beheld the room set with finest china and flatware. It glittered in the candlelight and she noted how the golden light that bathed everything did something magical to all it touched.

She was seated between Reginald and Olive, and looked to her aunt for guidance on what to do. Genevieve indicated Reginald and so she turned to him as the soup was placed before her.

"Do live in West Redditch, Mr. Haustman?"

"On the far side, yes. My father is Lord Faulkley, and we have a small estate called Mont Farlane."

"Oh yes? My father lives over in Withcombe."

"Any association with the famous Withcombe Bays?"

"You know of them?"

"Indeed I do! Own one—he is an amazing hunter."

"Oh, what is his name?"

"Withcombe Heart of Gold, but I call him Dan."

"Heart of Gold! But he was one of the first I helped with. He must be near nine years old now."

"I believe you are right. What do you mean, helped?"

Her mouth dropped open, for she did not know what to say. "Oh, I rode him a bit, and brushed him frequently. I loved the horses while I was there."

"I like them fine, though I am finding that my interests are shifting as I get older."

"Indeed. Grandfather says we will have a hunt sometime. Perhaps you will bring Heart of Gold when we do."

He smiled down upon her, and she noted her aunt gesturing for her to turn to Olive. She did so, saying, "I so enjoyed your playing. How long have you studied piano?"

"Oh, I messed up the first part. I always get so nervous and then I forget which chords I am supposed to play. But, to answer your question, I have played since I was very young. My mother has always insisted."

"But do you not enjoy it?"

Olive sighed and picked at her pheasant. "No, not so much. The harpsichord is fun because I like the sound it makes, but mother says it is vulgar. And, I was wretched at the harp. So…piano."

"Do you ride?"

"No. Mother says it is not elegant."

"Oh, if that is the case, then I would never wish to be elegant."

"You like horses?"

"Very much. There is nothing I love more than riding free across the fields."

Olive's hazel eyes lit up. "You make it sound so romantic."

Sarah ducked her head momentarily. "I don't know about that, but I do love to ride."

"I enjoy excursions in the carriage. Sometimes we will take a picnic out and sit by the lake. It is very peaceful."

"It sounds lovely. Do you dance?"

"Of course. Don't you?"

"I am still learning. I have not had much time to study it in my life."

"I wish I could say the same! Mother has had me with four different dancing masters, hoping one of them will make my feet more elegantly inclined. I'm afraid the problem isn't with the dancing masters, however."

"Well, you are better than me at any rate. I am overwhelmed with the sheer number of dances there are to learn."

"My goodness, yes! And it never fails but that I am asked to dance one I do not know so well!"

Sarah's eyes widened in sympathy. "I don't know what I shall do when that happens!"

"Just watch the couple at the top of the dance, they'll cue you in."

"I'll try."

The supper finished and the party began to break up. Sarah found herself feeling less lonely, somehow, as she went up to bed. Elsie met her and helped to undress her and get her into the linen nightgown and ruffled dressing gown. Then she picked up Sarah's clothes and carried them out, leaving her alone with a single candle. The light glinted on the silver combs, and she gave a small cry as she snatched them up before opening the door and looking outside. Elsie was gone.

She bit her lip and stepped into the hall. Her great-aunt's room was only a short way down the hall and she padded along, counting the doors as she went. She heard voices before she got there, and paused, recognizing her aunt and grandfather in heated discussion.

"...were you thinking inviting those people here?" Her grandfather sounded angry.

"Edmund, who am I supposed to invite?"

"She is the granddaughter of an earl..."

"And the daughter of a horse trainer. Think, Edmund. Your goal is to get her married creditably. We can only do that if she is introduced to society that will have her."

"The second son of a lord and a baronet's daughters?"

"Exactly. You must remember she is not Catherine."

"No. No, she is not. That is apparent."

The door opened and her grandfather stood there, looking stolid yet spare, firelight backlighting him and sparking silver upon his head. He pulled up when he saw her and his eyebrows knit together.

"What are you doing here?"

She held out the combs. "I'm simply returning these to Lady Genevieve…"

Her aunt took them gently. "Come, my dear, let's get you back to your room." She tossed a glance over her shoulder at Sarah's grandfather and led her off.

They reached the door to Sarah's room in silence. Sarah opened the door and made to enter when Genevieve stopped her. "I don't know what you heard, but I don't want you to think of it; do you understand?"

Sarah nodded without looking at her, and went inside. She sat on the edge of her bed, thinking. How did she feel about what she had heard? She didn't know, but something had changed and the light seemed to have gone out of her existence. Suddenly she wanted to be home in her tiny little room with her three dresses and her heavy work boots and mother's trunk. *Aitatxo* puttering about and the sound of stable lads out in the quad, and always the sound of horses—their nickers, whinnies, snorts, everything.

She didn't realize she was crying until something warm dripped onto her hand, then she lifted it and wiped the tears from her face. Being here was suddenly not possible; she could no longer take being an imperfect reminder of another person. Instead, she wanted to be home where she could be valued as she was, even if that meant pushing the duke aside so she could simply do her work.

She thought her heart might break, though. In that heart that felt ready to shatter, she had hoped that her aunt and grandfather would transform her into a person the duke could truly love. But instead…

She took off her dressing gown and nightdress. She

had to dig to find her old shift, but it was there at the bottom of the drawer with her old corset. They went on with relative ease, as did her old flannel petticoat and her long-sleeved blue dress. Her old stockings, the ones with the holes in the knees, and finally her old boots. She found the blanket that Emma had given her for the journey and arranged it around her shoulders like a shawl. Then, she opened her door and peered out.

The hall lay shrouded in darkness, and Sarah stepped out to duck silently along to the stairs. Carefully, she tip-toed down the countless steps until she reached the entrance hall below. By skirting the shadowed edges, she reached the door and pulled it open, cringing when it groaned. But she slipped free and pulled it closed running down the final steps and feeling her feet hit the grass of the front lawn.

Then she was off and running free. Ghostly shadows from the full moon lay everywhere in the freezing night. She rolled her hands into the blanket and hunkered down as she ran along the track toward the woods. They lay to the east, the direction of Withcombe.

Her lungs hurt from the cold air breathed in so rapidly as she raced, and by the time she reached the edge of the woods she had slowed to a walk. The exercise had warmed her, but she was winded as well. The branches of the trees obscured the moonlight and therefore the track. She stumbled along in near darkness, trying to get as far as possible before stopping to rest.

In the distance she heard water, and remembered passing over a bridge when they'd had their outing some weeks before. She bit her lip as she considered what she would do if she missed the bridge. Would she have to wait for daylight to find it?

Hours passed and her steps slowed as the temperature dropped even further. She tripped and fell down, scraping her hand on a stone and crying out. Somewhere in the distance a fox cried, almost as though answering her. She shivered a little as the cold penetrated through the layers surrounding her. With numbed fingers she pulled the blanket closer around her neck, ignoring the scratchy wool.

The sound of water grew nearer as she climbed a slight rise. All around her the woods were silent, as though waiting. Something crashed in the woods behind her, and she jumped, her footsteps lurching to a run as she stared through the darkness around her.

Suddenly the ground was gone and she was falling. Shocking cold struck her first, then sharp pain that caused her to cry out again.

She splashed through the river towards the far bank and pulled herself out, shaking and dripping. Her leg was not responding correctly and pain shot through it with each movement.

She crawled to an earthen overhang and curled up beneath it to wait for daylight.

If she did not freeze first.

Chapter Thirteen

It was late when William arrived into the town of West Redditch. The carriage pulled up to an inn and he climbed free, exhausted, though tempted to race off to Wrottlesby and demand to see Sarah. He had told no one of his plans and had simply packed clothes and ordered his carriage.

It had taken some time to find out where in Berkshire, Wrottlesby lay. Once found, it had been a simple endeavor to set off within the hour.

He climbed into the uncomfortable bed and rolled onto his back, staring at the unfamiliar ceiling and noting the corner where damp had seeped in. His candle was very nearly burnt out, so he reached over and extinguished it with one hand. The darkness around him felt oppressive, but on the morrow he would see Sarah and all would be well.

Showing up unannounced at Wrottlesby would be tantamount to declaring himself, but he no longer cared. He needed to see that she was all right, and try to determine her feelings for him. Also, how long she would remain in Berkshire…

He listened to the sleet coming down on the roof, and wondered how soon the damp spot would spread.

He was up early the next morning and ate an indifferent breakfast of gruel and lukewarm tea before ordering his carriage brought round. Though it was early for a call, he did not think he could wait much longer.

The horses pulled his carriage up to the door and he nodded to the postilion as he climbed inside. He tapped on the wall and they were off.

Wrottlesby lay in the countryside near a small lake. He barely noticed the countryside passing by until the manor house itself rose into view as they came around the edge of the forest. He nodded approvingly of its rambling wings and many chimneys smoking at that early hour.

The carriage stopped before the front steps and he waited for the groom to open the latch and let down the step. He swept down and then up the stairs to ring the bell.

A confused butler opened the door. "Yes, sir?"

"Please inform your master that the Duke of Tensington is here."

"Yes, sir. Please come in."

He noted the unusual tension in the shoulders of the butler and some tumult coming from up the stairs, even as he was whisked into a sitting room and bade to wait. Within moments, the old earl was there. Before William could say anything, the earl burst into speech,

"What have you done with her?"

"I beg your pardon?" William drew himself up.

"Sarah Mondragón is missing, and now you turn up. It is a strange coincidence."

"What do you mean missing?"

"Her maid just came to us saying her bed was not slept in and that her old clothes were missing. We cannot find her anywhere in the manor."

"But it froze last night! We must find her!"

"But…do you mean…she is not with you?"

"She is not. Did something happen? I understood she was happy here."

The earl's eyes were now large as he stared about the room in a daze. "Indeed, we must find her. My carriage!"

William ran out to where his carriage with the postilion waited. "Quickly, unhitch the horses. Give me the saddled one."

With a confused air, the postilion did as asked. As the horse was led up to William, the old fear rose in him but he battled it down. To distract himself, he asked, "Which horse is this one?"

"'Tis Bard."

"Ah. I know this horse."

The postilion adjusted the stirrups and William climbed up onto the back of the horse and set off. He stared around at the lay of the land and noted the well worn track leading off into the woods. It would have been dark—could she have been able to see? How much moon had there been? He urged the horse onward toward the road instead, thinking she would have taken the broader path away from Wrottlesby.

He fumbled a little with the reins and Bard slowed, his ears swiveling about in the morning light. After a moment, he had better control of the reins and urged Bard onward again. The horse broke into a bone-jarring trot down the track toward the woods and William fought desperately to post in time to his steps. The horse's head was up and his step quickened as the sound of a fox crying echoed from the woods.

He tried to slow the horse down, but Bard simply snatched his head free and headed off further down the track. He pulled on the leather reins to turn the horse's head but Bard resisted and ignored his directions. Then he broke into a canter and William had to struggle to find his seat and match the horse's rhythm.

A fox cried out again as the horse picked his way through the woods, going off the track at one point and into the trees. A low hanging branch nearly unseated William. He ducked down, clinging now to the pommel of the saddle and letting the horse choose its way.

The sounds of water grew closer, and he tensed. Bard seemed to sense this for his pace quickened slightly trotted over the uneven ground.

"Sarah! Sarah, where are you?" he called

The woods merely absorbed it. But a fox raspily called in response and Bard broke into a fast trot, pushing between the trees and through the undergrowth.

They plummeted suddenly, William lurching forward and nearly slipping off over Bard's neck before he righted himself. Then the horse plunged straight into the river and William had to pull his feet out of the stirrups to keep from getting wet. Then they were across and headed toward a sodden mound of rags.

It was Sarah.

He was off in a moment, Bard coming near and blowing hard.

"Your grace…"

"Sarah! Here, let's get you warm."

He pulled off his overcoat and wrapped her up in it. Then he lifted her from the ground and strained to place her on the horse. She helped instinctively, though she was nearly unconscious from cold. He adjusted her leg and she gasped in pain.

"It hurts…"

"We'll have you back at Wrottlesby soon."

"Take me to Withcombe. Please."

"I can't, my dear. We must get you warm. Your grandfather is worried."

He climbed up behind her, glad she couldn't see how ungainly he looked. He held her against him, trying to warm her with his body, and guided Bard back across the river and up the embankment.

Whatever sense had directed Bard to Sarah, William could only hope would guide him back. William was completely turned around, but knew if they got out of the woods he would be able to find his way back to the manor. But time was running out for Sarah...

Bard seemed to sense the urgency, for his steps came quickly, though William wavered in his balance upon the horse's back. Holding Sarah securely and managing the reins was more than he could handle, and once again, he let Bard have his head, only spurring him from time to time to underscore the urgency of their errand.

Bard needed little encouragement. He jogged smoothly along, picking his way across through the trees until they came to the wagon track. It was clearer here, and William breathed a sigh of relief. They had found their way...or rather, Bard had.

Soon enough they were climbing the slight rise to the manor house.

"Hello! Hello there!" William shouted as he neared the house.

The door opened as he approached and he yelled, "Quickly, get her to her room and warm her!" He lowered her down to the waiting arms of footmen and slid down to follow them.

They carried her slung between them, William's coat partly wrapped around her and dangling down onto the stairs as they went. He followed, noting her glazed, half-open eyes and fearing the worst.

"Quickly!" he cried.

The maid met them in the bedroom and they laid her before the fire which she had stoked. An elderly woman appeared and began giving directions.

"Elsie, help me get her out of these wet things. Get her nightdress and stockings ready. Your grace, please wait downstairs while we take care of her."

William left quickly, but stood outside the room listening to the two women's muffled voices and a soft cry he deduced was Sarah. He instantly pounded on the door.

"Her leg is injured. Please be careful!"

"Yes, your grace."

He paced, hardly seeing the paintings and carvings all around him. Finally, the door opened and he pushed past the old lady and the maid to the bedside. A maid came in with another blanket that was first warmed by the fire, then lowered over Sarah and tucked in while he chafed her icy hands, trying to warm them. Elsie appeared with the bed warmer.

"I just warmed it, not hot. Place 'er 'ands on it."

William did so, then covered them with his own to trap the warmth. "Sarah, say something." He groaned.

Her mouth moved and he bent near to hear a raspy, "Your grace…"

"If you please, ma'am, the doctor is here," The butler's announced in a solemn tone.

"Oh, excellent. Jarvis, have you sent men after my

brother?" The elderly lady asked.

"It is done, my lady."

Meanwhile, the doctor had roughly dislodged William and with an abrupt gesture, shooed everyone from the room except the old lady. William leaned against the door, eyes closed, as he waited once again.

He heard movement from within and straightened as the door opened and the old lady came out.

"Your grace, if you would come with me."

He entered the room where the doctor was packing his bag. Sarah's eyes were no longer staring blankly, but were closed and she appeared to be sleeping.

"Ply her with warm drinks. Do not let her sleep for long. When she is more alert, warm broth and milk, but nothing solid until I see her again." With a final glance at his patient, he left.

William looked at the lady who reached out to brush a tendril of hair from Sarah's face.

"She heard a part of a conversation my brother and I were having. She must have misinterpreted it and was hurt, to the point of running away. We did not know she had done so until this morning, shortly before you arrived."

"Who are you?"

She looked up at that, eyes wide open and eyebrows high in her forehead. "Oh, of course! We weren't introduced. I am Lady Genevieve Touillart, Sarah's great-aunt. I am the earl's sister."

Just then there was a slight commotion out in the hall and suddenly the earl stood there in the doorway. He approached slowly, one eye on William, and edged near to Sarah. He took one look at her and gasped, his gaze seeking his sister's.

"She is alive. The duke found her in time."

The elderly gentleman nearly collapsed with relief, and Elsie brought a chair forward for him. He buried his face in his hands and shook for a moment as if sobbing silently. Finally, he pulled a handkerchief from his pocket and wiped his eyes. He looked up at his sister and said, "I thought we'd lost her, too."

"I know, Edmund. But she is safe now. A bruised leg and near freezing, but the doctor thinks she will be all right."

He turned his wizened face to William. "And you, sir, what brings you to Wrottlesby?"

"I came to check on the wellbeing of Miss Mondragón."

"Ah. We have failed her in that. Thank God you were not too late."

"Yes."

With difficulty, the earl pushed himself up from the chair. "Your grace, you are wet. You need to dry yourself by the fire."

"I am more concerned for Miss Mondragón."

"I understand. But if you catch a fever you will be of no use to her."

William considered this, and with a glance back at Sarah, followed the old earl out. They went down the stairs to the sitting room where the fire had been stoked and he was waved into one of the chairs near the fireplace. The wet clothes had chilled him unaware, and he shivered a little, pulling closer to the heat.

The earl's hand rubbed the back of the chair he stood beside. "I will have tea and some refreshment sent in for you, and I will let you know when she wakens."

"Thank you. The horse I rode… it was he that found her. He must be cared for."

"I will send word to the stables that he is to be well looked after."

Then he was gone, and William was alone with his thoughts. If he had questioned his motives in coming here, he no longer did. The shock and fear of nearly losing Sarah had convinced him of what he had known all along—that he cared a little too much for Miss Mondragón.

And he did not know what to do with that…

Chapter Fourteen

A soft buzzing pierced the heaviness around her and she resisted it. It intensified and she tried to escape but it was insistent. Finally, her eyes opened to see three people hovering around her. And one of them was...

"William! I mean, your grace."

But he smiled, and the lines on his forehead disappeared as his eyes lit up and crinkled at the edge. "You may call me William."

"No your grace, but what are you doing here?" Her voice sounded strange and hoarse to her ears and she frowned.

"He came to check on you, and found you injured."

"Bard found you, I was just riding him."

"Bard...! He is here?"

"Indeed. I asked for the two best horses to pull the carriage, and he was one of them. He is in the stable now eating his fill of mash and whatever else horses like."

Sarah smiled. "I am glad." She turned to her grandfather and knew she needed to say something, but the words were difficult and she had to struggle with them. "Sir, I am sorry. I did not wish to be a burden to you."

"You are no burden, Sarah."

"But I am not my mother."

"And that is not a bad thing. I meant no disrespect of you as a person when I said that. I think a part of me wanted to get her back. But she is gone, and you are here. And I am slowly learning to be happy for that."

She nodded, but the movement hurt and she suddenly realized she was thirsty. In perfect timing, Elsie came in bearing a tray. Genevieve poured out a cup of tea, then put a large dollop of honey and brandy in it before holding it to Sarah's lips.

"Doctor says you must drink all we can give you."

Sarah sipped and frowned at the range of flavors in it. The brandy and the hot tea heated her up within and she sighed, but had to force herself to drink more. With a glance at the clock on the mantle, her grandfather patted her hand and rose, promising to check in on her later.

"Your grace, if you would come with me. I believe supper is ready. Genevieve?"

"I will be there, momentarily."

The two men left, William after a long look at Sarah who could not help but stare back. Her aunt fluttered around, feeling her forehead and chafing her hands.

"You are still cool to the touch. We must get you warmer. Elsie, stoke the fire more. I will be back to check on her after supper."

"Yes, ma'am." Elsie piled more coal onto the fire as Genevieve left and closed the door behind her.

Sarah sighed, relaxing backward into the pillow as Elsie collected the tray. "I'll take this downstairs. Do you want to try some broth?"

"Yes, that would be fine."

Elsie smiled at that and left, closing the door with

her foot. Sarah stared through her achiness at the little fire blazing for all it was worth. The duke was here…here! For her…so it seemed. What was she to make of that? She could hardly comprehend it and squeezed her eyes against the thought. There must be another explanation…

A knock and the door opened.

Elsie had returned, this time with a cup she set down on the nightstand. "Do you want to sit up and drink this time?"

Sarah nodded and pushed against the bed to rise, but made very little headway. Elsie held the cup to her lips as she drank the hot broth. It was comforting, somehow, and made her feel as though she had enjoyed an actual meal. When she had finished, she leaned back and sighed.

"That felt good."

"It does me good to see you. Oh, miss, you looked dead when they brought you in."

"Mmm. I don't remember anything after I fell into the river."

"It's a miracle you lived. His lordship said so."

"Well, I'm going to be fine, according to the doctor." Her voice still sounded hoarse and weak to her ears, however. Gradually, her breathing slowed and her eyes closed.

****

Something rattled, and then bright light shone through her eyelids. She scrunched her eyes closed tight and turned away.

"Miss, her ladyship is here with the doctor."

She groaned. A chill went through her and her head hurt, while her throat burned. She felt cool hands upon her forehead.

"She has a fever now. I was afraid of this. A latent humor has her in its grip. She must be bled."

"What?" Sarah stirred and tried to keep her eyes open.

The doctor was laying out some instruments even as Elsie appeared carrying a strange bowl with a section cut out of it. The doctor laid her arm upon it and with a sudden stab, there was a piercing pain in the crease of her elbow.

She cried out, but was ignored by the doctor, who held a small cup with a brownish substance to her lips. She drank the bitter concoction and made a face, even as the world tipped all of a sudden.

She drifted, as cold ice stabbed through her and left her pierced and bleeding…all her blood draining away leaving her white and empty and cold.

She shivered roughly and someone held another cup to her lips.

"Drink, now, my dear. This will help."

But the bitter fluid ran down her throat and she choked as though she were drowning.

The river. She struggled through the water even as it rose over her, forcing her to gulp air between waves. Then she sank…sank into a burning cauldron…

****

She woke. Her nightgown was damp and cool. Slumped in the chair beside her was the duke, while curled on the floor beside the fire lay Elsie. Sarah raised a hand to her face and found it damp as well, her hair clinging to her skin. Weakly, she pushed herself up until she was sitting.

The duke's eyes opened and he reached for her.

"Lie down. You had a bad go of it."

Elsie stirred and lifted her head, "Oh, miss, you're awake!"

"So it would seem. What happened?"

The duke pushed her gently back onto the pillows. "Lie still for a while. You need to take it slowly. You've been very ill."

She relaxed against the pillow and the door opened to admit her aunt. Her faded blue eyes widened as she caught sight of Sarah and she smiled, one hand going to her throat.

"Oh my dear, such a wonderful sight!" She felt Sarah's forehead then turned to Elsie. "You must bathe her and get her in a clean nightdress. Your grace, with me if you please."

With a backward glance at Sarah, the duke followed her out .

Elsie returned with a steaming basin and a towel and set to washing Sarah gently as though she were a sickly kitten, which was not far from the truth. Afterward, she lowered a warmed and dry nightgown over her head and helped her into the chair with a blanket over her lap. Then she quickly changed the bed linens. By that time, Sarah's strength was giving out and she was happy to be helped back into bed. She sank back with a sigh onto the dry, warm, bed.

Genevieve appeared with her grandfather and the duke towering over them. Elsie left with an armful of dirty linens and clothes then returned with a tray containing tea and toast with jam.

Sarah was helped back into a sitting position with pillows rearranged to support her, then the tray set carefully on her lap. She ate and drank slowly, but found she was hungry. The tea had been sweetened with honey and lemon, and the toast heavily buttered. She enjoyed it all.

When she had finished, Elsie removed the tray and disappeared, leaving the duke, her aunt, and grandfather encircling her. The duke reached for her hand lying on the coverlet and she smiled at him, then looked up at her grandfather who had a tear in his eye.

"It is good to see you awake and a…ware."

She was sure he had nearly said 'alive.'

"Thank you, Grandfather. I am sorry to have been such trouble."

"No trouble, my dear. Just worried, very worried."

"How is Bard?"

"He was well last night when I checked in."

"Does my father know?"

The duke cleared his throat. "I wrote to him of your illness. Just now I told him your fever had broken and that you were well."

"Oh good. He will fret…"

"We all did. You were quite ill, Miss Mondragón."

"I am sorry."

"None of that, my dear," her aunt said. Then she looked up at the cluster of caring faces and added, "We should leave her to rest. Come your grace, Edmund…"

Sarah watched them go and sighed. Warmth flowed not only over her, but through her as she remembered the expressions on each of their faces as they had looked at her.

Her eyes closed, and she drifted off.

Chapter Fifteen

William followed the earl and his sister from the room, glancing back once more to see Sarah's gaze upon him. Those eyes were awake and alive. Relief and something else warm and vivid, and almost painful washed through him at the sight. Could it be he was in love?

He tried to push the thought from his head, but it persisted. The simplistic infatuations he had experienced in the past were nothing like this. This feeling left him breathless, yet wanting more...

He followed the earl to the sitting room where Lady Touillart rang for tea. Personally, he wanted something stronger than tea, but he would settle for whatever drink was closest to hand. Lady Touillart settled next to a low table where the tray was set when it was brought. She poured out a cup and handed it to him black.

"Thank you," he said, but did not drink right away. He stared at the fire for a moment, thinking of Sarah lying in her bed, hair clinging wetly to her face...

"How long do you intend to stay, now that we are reassured of Sarah's health?" the earl asked.

William shifted his attention to him and shrugged. "I don't want to be any trouble. I could leave today if you so desired."

"Nonsense. We have no fixed engagements. I was

just curious. You appear devoted to our little Sarah, and we naturally wonder what your intentions are."

His eyebrows shot up. "My…intentions…are honorable. I merely wish to see her returned to health and happy. I can see she is well cared for."

"Indeed, we have done our best." But the earl frowned when he said this, and his lips compressed. "At least, we have done what we thought was best."

"If you would indulge me, I would like to stay until she is up and about so I can give her father a good report."

"Of course, of course. As I said, it is no trouble."

The company lapsed into silence, then William said, "I met your daughter, once, when I was a boy."

The earl looked up, interested. "Oh, yes?"

"Yes. I was playing in the gallery, when I heard the most wonderful music coming from somewhere in the manor. I sought it out, and found a beautiful lady playing the pianoforte in the parlor. Hiding by the door was my father, who shushed me when I went to ask who she was. The song ended and she rose to leave, but caught sight of us standing there. She spoke to me—I don't remember what she said, but I remember being quite transfixed."

"She was very talented. I hope she was able to keep it up."

"I cannot say I ever heard it again, but then I was away at school much of the time."

Genevieve nodded. "I believe Sarah has inherited her mother's talent, though she is still early in her training. Something about the way she handles the keys reminds me of Catherine."

William placed his empty cup in its saucer and

stood. "If you will excuse me, I will go check on the horses and my man. Sarah will want to know they are well when she wakens."

The cold, crisp air assaulted him as he stepped free of the house. The stables stood near the main house, and he gladly moved into the slightly less icy interior. He went to the stalls where his horses were being boarded and found Bard standing in one corner, dozing by the look of it. His head jogged up when the duke spoke to him and he nickered softly, ambling over to the door. William spent a moment patting him. The old fears were loosening their grip upon him, and he almost felt like going for a ride.

He pushed aside the feeling and checked on the other horse who looked like he could be Bard's brother. The postilion had called him Roger, and William spent a moment patting him as well. When he looked up, his postilion stood there, cap in hand.

"The 'orses is doin' well, yer grace," the man said.

"So I see. Have they recovered from the trip?"

"Aye, sir. They're fit."

"Good. We may be leaving in a day or two."

"Yes, sir."

William's step quickened as he neared the manor and entered the main door. The air in the house was warmed and did not hurt to breathe as the air outside had. He made his way up the stairs to Sarah's room and knocked gently, only to hear "Come in."

He opened the door to find Sara sitting up beside the fireplace, swathed in her dressing gown and with stockings upon her feet. Her hair had just been washed, and Elsie was slowly combing it out and drying it in the warmth of the fire. Her damp hair made her eyes look larger and more childlike, and he felt the unfamiliar lurch in his chest again.

"You're up!"

She smiled, and he noticed she had a little more color. "Yes, thanks to Elsie. She is determined to see me well!"

"Then we are all indebted to her."

"Are you staying long at Wrottlesby?"

"Another day or two to see you up and about. I would like to take a good report back to your father when I go."

"Dear *Aitatxo*! He will have been so worried…"

"As we all were. You were quite ill."

"Well, I am better now. I am even hungry!"

"That is excellent news. I will tell your aunt, and I am sure she will send a plate of something up for you."

"Thank you."

He hesitated, but there was nothing more he could say. He nodded to her and backed from the room, shutting the door as he went. He stood there for a moment, leaning against it, then turned to make his way to his own quarters. Once there, he rang for a servant.

"I shall be leaving tomorrow. Please see that my bag is packed and my brown suit is brushed and ready."

"Yes, your grace."

William strode to the parlor where Genevieve still sat. She was quietly playing something on the piano, though it was evidently hurting her fingers as she kept stopping to massage them.

"This rheumatism! I can't do half the things I used to."

"My father was afflicted with it. I know it was difficult for him to walk late in life."

Grace Colline

"I thank God I am still able to walk well. It is mostly my fingers, which is bad enough."

"Sarah states she is hungry. Also, I have instructed the servants to have my things ready to go tomorrow. Thank you for your hospitality."

"You must thank Edmund; this is his house. He simply allows me to live here now. My husband left me with nothing but a title." She rang the bell, then instructed the servant to arrange for a tray to be sent up.

"I'm sorry, ma'am." William said.

"No, no. It was a happy marriage. He simply had no head for business and people took terrible advantage of him. When he died, the estate had to be sold to pay his debts. But, I was able to keep my clothes and my jewelry, and Edmund insisted I come live with him. So, a happy ending."

"I can see that. This seems to be a happy home."

She frowned a little. "Ye..es. Perhaps not always, but certainly since Sarah has come. She has breathed life into this old place."

"Yes, Withcombe is a sadder place without her."

"I understand Sarah lives with her father in a cottage."

"It is a small, but comfortable home, from what I have seen."

"She is a talented horsewoman."

"Indeed, yes. I don't think there is anything she can't do with them."

A little silence fell and William stared off into nothing for a moment.

"Excuse me, please. The last few days…weeks even…have been quite heavy with anxiety."

"Yes. I can see that." Her sharp eyes pierced him

120

through, and he squirmed a little under her gaze. "What do you envision for her future?"

William looked into the faded blue eyes. "That will be for Sarah to determine."

"I see." Genevieve's smile faded.

William stood, unable to wait any longer. "Will you accompany me to her room to see how she is doing?"

Genevieve sighed. "These old legs are tired. I will sit here, if you don't mind."

"Of course. I won't be long."

The hall echoed with his footsteps as he strode along past servants bustling about their duties. Doors opened and closed up and down the hallway, and he went unerringly to Sarah's door and knocked.

A breathless, "Come in," followed and he pushed the door open.

Sarah stood in a golden brown dress with her hair twisted up neatly and tendrils curled loosely about her face. She leaned on a cane, however, and William frowned in concern.

"Should you be up? Your leg…!"

"It is getting better. The doctor says it was not broken. See.," She took a step forward, but the stick slid out from her grasp and she fell.

He caught her in his arms before she hit the floor. Her face turned to his, tantalizingly close, and before he could think, he claimed her lips with his own.

A gasp and a crash separated them. Elsie stared at them in the midst of shattered crockery. William made sure that Sarah was stable before excusing himself.

He left quickly, up the hall to his own room where he shut the door securely behind him. His bed had been made and his brown suit hung clean and brushed, for the morrow. He leaned against the window and closed his eyes.

Damn and blast! What was it that kept him going back to her? He had kissed her again, and the servant had witnessed it! What was he to do?

His eyes opened and he knew what he must do. He must leave and try to get over these feelings he carried. Somehow he must get the better of this. It was either that or…he could not face the alternative. He was not ready for marriage in any case…and what would people think? Did he even care?

He didn't know. Confused scenarios played through his mind. One moment he married her, the next he didn't, the next he presented her to friends in town and weathered their cutting remarks.

What was he to do?

Every cell of his being cried out to withstand the sea of ridicule and marry her, but there lay that splinter of fear festering in his soul. He heard his mother's voice blasting Sarah and her connections and working to make her life miserable. Perhaps the best thing to do if he loved Sarah…

Love? Is that what this was? Was he then to live without it? He could not envision this coming again for him. And yet…was it fair to subject Sarah to the judgment and ridicule that would come from so many directions?

He closed his eyes tightly against the thought.

Without a word, he dressed quickly in his travelling suit and packed his bag. Then he rang the bell and instructed the servant to call his carriage. He watched out the window until he saw it pull around the front, then he went downstairs to meet it.

"Go as far as we can today."

"Yes sir," he said as he shut the door.

Staring out the window, he watched the countryside slip past. A tightness at the back of his throat threatened to burst forth in a show of emotion that he was resolved against. He would not break; he would leave her and set her free.

And though he thought his heart might break, it continued to beat.

Chapter Sixteen

Sarah stood looking blankly at the door where William had disappeared. Another kiss—this one deeper and more meaningful, filled with desire and longing. It had taken her breath away.

But where had he gone?

She sat back in the chair beside her fire, not trusting herself to walk far in her present state. Her heart hammered blindly about like a bird desperate to escape a cage. She clutched the head of the cane and leaned forward on it.

From the doorway came the sounds of crockery being picked up and swept. Elsie had not said anything yet, and Sarah wondered if she would. At any rate she would be thinking about it and might even tell her aunt. Oh no…

"Elsie."

"Miss?" Elsie paused with a clay shard in her hand.

"Please, don't tell my aunt or anyone what you saw…"

"No, miss."

"Thank you. Can you close the door?"

"Yes, miss."

The door shut out most of the sounds coming from the hallway and down the stairs. She had originally planned to go down to supper, but now she could not face that. She could only sit and go over in her head the image of his face coming closer, the feel of his lips moving upon her, the sensations that had awakened...

A tiny groan escaped her.

She rose a little unsteadily and went to the window. The duke's carriage appeared from around the back where the stables were located. Her brow creased. Then the duke came out the front doors and got into the carriage. It jolted forward and headed off toward West Redditch.

The duke was leaving? But why?

There was only one reason she could think of, and it like to cut her through. He did not want her. But had she done something wrong when they kissed? Perhaps she wasn't good enough...

That was it. She was simply the granddaughter of an earl, and the daughter of a horseman, and that would not do for a duke.

Slowly she made her way back to the fireside, suddenly unutterably weary. The door opened and her aunt entered.

"Sarah, the butler just informed me that the duke has left. Is this true?"

"I saw him go just now."

"I knew he was leaving in the morning, but I thought he had intended to stay another night."

"I don't know, Aunt. He came to see me, then the next thing...I saw him driving off in his carriage."

Genevieve's eyes narrowed. "Did anything happen when he was here?"

Sarah's mouth dropped open, but no sound came out.

"I see. Then perhaps it is for the best."

"Oh Aunt..."

Genevieve pulled her close for a moment. "I know, dear. It will get better with time."

She sniffed, then nodded. "Yes, ma'am."

"I will let you be, but don't brood for too long."

"No."

Genevieve patted her cheek and left. Elsie bustled in and added another lump of coal on the fire, glancing once at Sarah. "Is there anything I can get for you, miss?"

"No, Elsie. Thank you. I'll be going down for supper."

An hour later when the gong had rung, Sarah rose with help from the cane and Elsie and made her way down to the dining room. She was listless, her feet heavy and graceless. The injury to her leg ached the longer she was up on it and it became ever more difficult to walk. It was with relief she reached her chair in the oak-paneled room where the long table stood.

Her grandfather smiled at her and she tried to smile back. But nothing felt right, for the duke had gone.

"I am making plans for our hunt," he said.

"Oh, excellent," Genevieve said.

"Yes, indeed," Sarah managed to say.

"You will need to practice jumps riding sidesaddle."

She nodded. "How will I do that?"

"We can set up some low fences for you to jump over. Arthur is supposed to be good at all that. I'm negotiating the hounds and the master of the hunt and who-all is needed."

"Excellent," she said. "That sounds like great fun. Perhaps Lavinia will join us."

"Yes, there are others I'd like to introduce you to

as well."

She put her spoon down next to her empty bowl. "Like who?"

"Just some other people you will not have met as yet. A couple of families who live near here and who are great sportsmen and women."

Genevieve's mouth compressed and she put her spoon down.

Sarah noted this and was suddenly hesitant. She suspected these people might be the people her great-aunt had chosen not to introduce her to. She understood her aunt's reasoning, though people's parents and background meant nothing to her personally. It was important in some spheres for people to stick to their own stratum. She just wasn't sure what that was for her.

Her grandfather evidently thought it was higher than her aunt thought. The uncertainty made her nervous, and strangely she longed for the duke even more...

William.. He is William, Duke of Tensington. Why could that not suffice? She as Sarah, he as William, two people drawn to one another through no fault of their own. Held apart by the difference in station between them.

She looked at the piece of roast venison and suddenly had no appetite. And yet, there would be comment and worry if she did not eat. Sighing silently, she picked up her knife and fork and cut a small piece off. It was savory and tender, beautifully cooked and yet she could not enjoy it. She set her fork and knife down.

"You're not eating, Sarah? Is something wrong with your venison?"

"No, it is perfect. I'm just not terribly hungry right now."

"Doctor said to feed you up, so eat what you can." Grandfather pointed his fork at her plate and she picked up her utensils again.

Had the duke stopped for the night? How far had he planned to go that day? Why does he not come back and kiss her like he did?

Grandfather was speaking. "And I thought we could have a little ball. Nothing extensive, just a few families. Get all the young people together—give them something to do."

"Sarah will need a new dress."

"Well, you should enjoy that! Dress her up fine as you can, get the dancing master to get her up to speed." He smiled at her again and she forced one for him.

It wasn't until she was alone in her room that she could cry in silence for the duke.

****

It was early the next day when Arthur was brought round, saddled and bridled and prancing. A low barrier had been set up on the lawn, and once again her aunt and grandfather sat where they could watch Sarah's progress.

First, she rode in a large circle, starting at a walk, and ending with a canter, all executed smoothly. Then she steered Arthur toward the pole set up in the midst of the lawn and readied herself to anticipate the horse's movements and the shifting of balance as he jumped over the fence.

He leapt over it easily, and she found herself nearly sliding off the right side. Angry with herself, she tried it again and again until she jumped it perfectly, then she rode up to her grandfather and aunt. Both she and Arthur were breathing hard from exertion.

"I admire your tenacity, my dear," said the earl.

"Yes, indeed. The last few jumps were perfect," her aunt said.

"I'd like it set higher, if possible," Sarah said.

"We'll see what can be done. Why don't you go for an easy ride about the park while I arrange it?."

"Yes, Grandfather."

She reined Arthur about with relief. The thought of being alone for a little time made her nearly sob out loud. She guided him toward the woods, then followed its edge for a time. She knew it had taken her nearly three days to get from Withcombe to Wattlesby, so William was somewhere in between now. Was he thinking of her? Did he long for her the way she longed for him? Surely not, or he would not have left so quickly.

She pushed Arthur into a slow canter and rode out toward a low building in the distance. Arthur's ears pricked forward and he loped willingly along. The crisp air flowed past her face, smarting her eyes. Tears leaked out the edges.

The low building resolved into a series of thatched buildings—a cottage and two barns. A wide-eyed girl paused scrubbing clothes in a tub.

"'Ello, miss."

"Good morning. I seem to have stumbled on a farm."

"Aye, miss. Gurkin Farm of Wattlesby. My father is Ted Gurkin."

"And who are you?"

"Polly. Polly Gurkin."

"I am Sarah Mondragón. I'm staying with my grandfather at Wattlesby."

"Oh yes! My sister is in service there. In the kitchen."

"What is her name?"

"Dora Gurkin."

"I shall have to look her out. I'd best be going, good day, Polly."

"Good day, miss."

Sarah reined Arthur around and headed back toward the manor. Did William have tenants? Did he know them? He had been gone for so long, and yet farmers were often there for generations. Suddenly she was curious. She had grown up at Withcombe, and yet knew very little of the surrounding farms save how much hay and oats they produced.

Urging her horse into a canter, she pushed him to a gallop as they neared the manor. She raced him toward the jump that had been set up and held her breath as they took it full speed.

Arthur cleared it well and they continued on for half a mile before she pulled him into a slow jog and headed back.

Genevieve's hand lay on her chest, fluttering. "Oh, my dear, that was thrilling. And yet I don't know that I ever want to see you do that again!"

"Nonsense! She's a born horsewoman! Can't wait to see her in the hunt."

A groom came forward and Sarah dismounted, spending a moment getting reacquainted with the ground. The three of them strolled together back to the manor where Genevieve rang for tea. It was brought and Sarah savored the drink, pouring a second cup immediately after drinking her first.

"You have color in your cheeks. It is good to see," the earl said.

"I am feeling mostly well, now."

"We have secured you an invitation to a ball being held at Crattsmore, an estate over near Denby. It will be in a week, so hopefully Miss Van Welder will get the dress done in time."

"What does it look like?"

"Ah! That will be a surprise."

Chapter Seventeen

The Dowager Duchess of Tensington sat bolt upright on the settee nearest the fire. William slouched on the opposite one, arms folded and staring into the flames.

"How are you set for coals?"

"There's plenty, Mother."

"But are you sure? Winter is coming and it will be more difficult to get…"

"I have checked with Hinckley and she agrees that we have enough coal."

"Well, then, that should be all right. Did the kitchen put by enough jams and onions and potatoes?"

"Mother, surely there are servants whose job it is to know these things?"

"It is your responsibility to know everything that is going on with your estate. I have found several issues with Marwinne and have only just started to set them right."

William felt a moment of pity for his former staff.

"Are you set for a wife, yet?"

"Mother, it isn't that easy."

"Of course it is. Find a girl of appropriate breeding and ask her. She'll say yes and there you are."

"She might say no." He thought of Sarah's pride and his lips compressed.

"There, what was that look for? You've found

someone. Well, who is it?"

"There's no one."

"Whoever it is—"

"I said, *there's no one*." He buried his head in his hand. "I don't wish to discuss it. Please."

A sullen silence followed, but William relished it. The duchess had been picking at everything since she arrived. He suspected she secretly missed being in charge of Withcombe and took out her frustration in constant criticism. At any rate, he was tired of it.

The gong sounded and William stood, belatedly remembering to offer his arm to his mother. She took it and they progressed to the dining room where the footman seated her and the first course was brought in.

His first sip of the turtle soup told him it was weak, and he braced himself for another comment from his mother. She said nothing, however, simply took a few spoonfuls and set her spoon aside.

"What sorts of amusements do you have?"

"What do you mean?"

"Parties and balls and such."

"I had a ball a few months ago when the Marchioness of Lilsbury was here. And I just returned from a visit to Berkshire."

"What is in Berkshire?"

"Wrottlesby."

Her fork clattered on the plate. "Wrottlesby...that's where that girl came from! That...Catherine! What business have you with those people?"

"The earl's granddaughter lived here for most of her life, then went to live with him. I wanted to make sure she was settled well."

"A letter would not suffice?"

"Why do you care? You keep wanting me to get out and meet people. I did."

"But they have a scandalous association with us. I forbid it!"

"I'm well over the age when I need permission with whom I consort."

"With whom are you consorting?"

He sighed forcefully. "No one. It was a figure of speech."

"You should be spending your time with people of your rank and station. That is where you will find a wife."

He wondered what would happen if he introduced the idea of marrying Sarah... Nothing good, he was sure.

"I'm not ready for that as yet. There is plenty of time. What would you like to do while you are here?"

"I have missed my card parties. I don't suppose one would be possible?"

"Of course. Shall I leave you to arrange it?"

"Yes, that will be all right. Hinckley and I will take care of it."

A little distraction for his mother would be welcome. Anything to keep her from sticking her nose into the running of the estate.

As soon as they were done with supper, she rang for the housekeeper and left. His mother's strident tones faded into the distance. He sat with his glass of port, which he disliked. He only took it when his mother was present, and he decided it was time to stop. She could say what she liked, he would not be hidebound by tradition.

He rose, trying to think what to do. More foals had

been born, and he decided to walk down and see them. Perhaps there would be a letter from Sarah…

The air bit his lungs as he breathed. Clouds encircled his head and he drew the collar of his overcoat up. The grass crunched underfoot as he strode down to the stables, lit with warm lights from within.

William entered the quad and headed straight for the broodmares' stalls. He held the lantern up to see the first foal standing pressed up against its mother's side. It was too dark to note if it were a colt or filly, but he smiled and moved on to the next one. He worked his way down, noting there were five now housed in the stable, and wondering where the others had gone. He made his way back to the entrance to the quad and patted Bard as he nickered, his head over the door.

"Hello, old fellow. Are you missing her too?"

The gelding was now in the place of honor. Blue had been moved out to pasture and once Arnas had heard the story of Bard finding Sarah, nothing was too good for the horse.

"Your grace?" Arnas stood on his little porch, with Zigor at his knee.

"Yes, Mondragón. Just looking at the horses."

"Do you want to come in? We have a few more to name."

"Tomorrow, perhaps. I won't disturb you tonight."

"Yes sir."

The door closed, and William wondered why he felt so awkward when all he wanted was to know how Sarah was doing.

He made his way up the hill and into the manor where he shed the overcoat and headed into the parlor. His mother sat bolt upright on the settee and he poured himself a brandy before settling in the chair beside the fire.

"Did you find out what you wanted to know?"

He frowned. "What do you mean?"

"You have shown far too much interest in that horse girl."

Irritation prickled him and he shifted uncomfortably beneath her gaze. "I am concerned about all my tenants."

"Name them."

"What?"

"Give me three names of tenants."

"Err…McGruder…"

"McGrale."

"Pitt?"

"Yes."

"I'm still learning the rest."

"It's been months. What have you been doing?"

"Figuring out the horse business."

"And what is your conclusion?"

"It brings in income. The horses are valuable."

"So your father thought. I could never see it."

"Withcombe Bays are excellent hunters and carriage horses. They are attractive and reliable. Good value."

"As long as they carry their share of the burdens of this estate."

"They do."

She went silent, but after a moment looked hard at him. "And the horse girl?"

"Is visiting her grandfather, the earl, as I said. I don't know if or when she is coming back."

"Her being gone is for the best. It sounds as though

she distracts you."

He picked up a poker and stabbed at the fire. How would he endure another week of his mother's presence? At least the following night she would be having her card party so he would be off the hook for that.

As though reading his mind, she asked, "Are you joining us tomorrow?"

"I think not. I may be going over some accounts with the steward."

"Oh, is it still Rafferty?"

"Of course."

"It is not uncommon for people to change stewards when they inherit. Shortsighted practice to my mind."

"Yes, well, I don't know the estate well enough to even consider it. Rafferty seems trustworthy."

"Your father certainly thought so."

William set the empty brandy glass down and stood. "Well, good night, Mother."

Her eyebrows rose, but she simply nodded and looked away.

****

The next morning brought a letter from Maggie:

My Dearest Tensington!

You will never guess where I am! In London, not half a day away from you. I find myself without a horse, my last one having twisted something inside—a bowel or something, and had to be put down. So I thought I would simply come and buy one of yours. Surprise! I will be there on Saturday and if you can, could you put me up for a day or two?

Your friend,

Maggie

William thought fast—what did they have that would be suitable for a woman like Maggie? His next thought was to wonder how his mother would get along with her. At any rate, he had but a day to get ready for Maggie's arrival so he summoned Hinckley.

She sailed into the dining room in somber gray, chatelaine tinkling at her side. William wondered again how old she was—she seemed positively ageless and yet had been there for years. He quickly put the situation before her and she simply nodded.

"It will be taken care of, your grace." Then she sailed out to handle everything.

William dressed and headed down to the stables to discuss the possible sale with Arnas. The old horsemaster sat in the sun, calling to stable boys as they went by and checking on their work. He looked up as William approached and fell silent.

"Mondragón."

"Duke Tensington."

"I have a friend coming in a day or two who wishes to buy a horse. Do we have any available?"

"Describe your friend to me."

"She is tallish, blonde hair, blue eyes…"

Arnas closed his eyes and said, "I mean her needs as a horsewoman. Hunter, carriage…?"

"Ah. Hunter, I believe. And for general riding."

"We have two that would suit. I will have them groomed and clipped to show her. Henry!" he called to the young man in the nearby ring, who instantly came over. "Get Top and Tilt ready to be shown this weekend."

"Yes, sir."

"I was afraid you would say Bard."

"With your blessing, Bard goes nowhere."

"I agree with you. Have you heard from your daughter lately?"

Arnas's expression closed off, but he said, "Yes, she does well. She is riding and going to suppers and balls and who knows what else. She misses us and the horses of course. I don't know that she likes being a fine lady."

"Your daughter is filling the role beautifully, as I can attest." He nodded and turned away, stopping to pat Bard as he went by.

His mind was taken with a series of images of Sarah. Her lying wet and frozen on the ground, her glazed eyes when he laid her on the bedroom floor, and then her glorious transformation dressed and looking like a goddess in his eyes.

The now familiar longing struck him and he struggled against it.

He paused in his walk, halfway to the manor. Breathing hard, and not all of it from walking, he leaned on one knee and begged whatever gods might be listening to make it so he could be with her.

Something moved at the window and he frowned. Even from that distance he recognized his mother watching him. He stood and breathed out a heavy breath before continuing on.

After his overcoat was taken, he made his way to the parlor where his mother was waiting. She had not moved from the window and did not acknowledge him when he came in. He sat in one of the chairs.

"We'll have another guest in a day or two. The Marchioness of Lilsbury, Magdalene Umphert. She wants to look at a couple of horses."

"Do you need me to cut my stay short?"

"No, Mother. Stay as long as you want."

"Good. The drains at Marwinne have had to be dismantled and replaced. I am told the smell is quite overpowering. I may need to stay some weeks until the job is done."

"Of course, Mother. You are no trouble."

****

The next day brought Maggie. She swept in, her shawl and the feathers in her hat fluttering. She kissed William on the cheek, and curtseyed very prettily before his mother who seemed instantly taken with her. Mildred had been left behind.

"Your grace, so good of you to share your son's hospitality with me."

"Nonsense. We must help our friends. I'm only too glad you thought of Withcombe for your horse."

Maggie smiled graciously and turned to William. "Shall we walk down and look at them? I want to see all Withcombe has to offer!"

William motioned her to the door. She took his arm, though he had not offered it and forced him to walk beside her. Uncomfortable with the arrangement, he tested how firmly she had hold of him and determined it would be rude to shake her free.

Together, they strolled down to the stables and into the quad. As soon as they appeared, the stable boys and grooms took up their places in front of the horses' stalls and stood at attention. William was surprised, but left Maggie looking at Bard while he went to the cottage. Arnas came stumping to the door and out into the gray day.

"If your grace would like to sit on the bench, we

will bring out the horses."

"Of course. Maggie, come here. They are going to bring them out."

"What about this one?" She patted Bard's neck.

Arnas shot a nervous look at William.

"That one is not for sale."

With a little *moue* that was intended to melt hearts, she turned from Bard and made her way over to William. Soon enough the horses were led out into the large exercise ring before them.

"Withcombe Top o' the Morning." Arnas said as the first horse, a reddish bay, stepped lightly by with head up and pricked ears, listening in all directions at once.

He was saddled and Henry climbed up, showing how well he responded to commands. His neck had a lovely arch to it as he cantered along. There was a low jump in the ring and he went over it flawlessly. Then the second horse was brought out.

Arnas gestured to him. "Withcombe Tilting Knave."

This horse was darker, more sedate in his movements. He jumped fluidly and cantered, with a slight arch to his neck and long lines through his body.

When both had been exhibited, the saddle was changed out for a sidesaddle and Maggie was invited onto Top first. It took her a moment to settle her skirts, then she picked up the reins and rode sedately around the ring before urging the horse to a canter. She rode in a figure eight, then took the horse over the low jump and cantered up to the fence.

"He's very nice!" she said as she slipped down.

The second horse was taller by half a hand and it

took a little longer for her to mount. She rode him much the same way as the other, however when she attempted the jump, she lost her balance and tipped forward off the horse on landing.

William jumped up and raced into the ring while Henry ran to capture the horse. He skidded to his knees beside the still form of Maggie and gently turned her face up. Her eyes were shut and when he went to move her she groaned. There was a slight reddened area on her forehead and her gown was torn but other than that no other damage could be seen.

He caught Arnas's gaze. "Send for a doctor!"

"It is done."

"Have someone help me get her into the house."

A stable lad came forward. Between them they carried Maggie's limp body into the cottage and arranged her on the sofa. She groaned again and he bent near to see if she said anything.

"William," she whispered.

William paced to one side until the doctor arrived in his carriage. Over an hour had passed, and still Maggie had not wakened. Doctor White very quickly took out his smelling salts and waved it under her nose.

She coughed and her eyes fluttered open. Her gaze sought out William's and she said weakly, "Oh, your grace, what happened?"

"You fell from the horse, don't you remember?"

"No, that is unlike me. Are you sure?"

"Quite sure. How do you feel?"

The doctor hushed them as he listened to her heart and breathing, checked her eyes and felt her limbs. "I can find no damage, but—"

"My head hurts, and feels weak. Is it possible I hit

it?"

"You have a red mark, and may have a brain contusion. We will have to keep you quiet for a few days and see if you get stronger."

"Would it be safe to move her to the manor?"

"I believe so. We can take her in my carriage. Keep her warm and quiet."

"Can you walk?"

"I don't know…"

She clung to him as he supported her up, then collapsed against him, eyelids fluttering. They opened again before the doctor could use his salts and she said "I don't think I can. I'm so sorry."

William said nothing, simply bent and lifted her up to carry her to the carriage. He set her on the seat and stood back for the doctor to enter. Maggie leaned against the side of the carriage, eyes closed.

"I'll meet you up there."

William set off immediately and was nearly to the manor by the time the carriage passed him on the little road. He trotted the rest of the way and pulled in time to tell the butler to call footmen to carry Maggie up to her room. As he watched her go, he rubbed his forehead with his palm and closed his eyes. Things had just gotten complicated.

He encountered his mother on the stairs and she stopped him with a bejeweled hand.

"What is going on? I saw a pair of servants carrying that young woman of yours up the stairs."

"She's not my young woman. She fell off a horse and hit her head. God knows how long for her to convalesce."

"Is her head right?"

"We don't know. Right now she is light-headed and cannot stand. We shall have to see how she does overnight."

His mother turned and glided up the stairs, no doubt to supervise their guest's care.

William covered his face with his hand and prayed that Maggie was all right.

Chapter Eighteen

Sarah sat waiting for Elsie to bring in the ball gown from her aunt's room. Footsteps sounded in the hall outside and her heart jumped, then Great-Aunt Genevieve entered with a gown draped over her arms.

Of a deep, twilight blue silk, its bodice was short and edged at the neckline with cream and blue silk twisted with a fine string of pearls. A cream inset was edged with thin silver lace and the sleeves were of blue silk slashed to show the cream silk underneath. Sarah had never seen anything so lovely.

Elsie immediately arranged it so that she could step inside and the dress was drawn up around her. It was fastened at the back and she turned around to look at herself in the mirror.

She hardly recognized herself. An elegant young lady stood there, not the daughter of Arnas Mondragón. Panic welled up and she shook her head.

"I can't do this," she said.

Genevieve's hands fell firmly on her shoulders without disturbing the dress. "Yes you can, my dear. You will simply need to dance a few dances and make sure you don't spill any punch. Oh, and talk nicely to the other participants. That is all."

Her heartbeat slowed somewhat and she allowed her aunt to draw her downstairs to where the carriage waited. Her grandfather was there and he smiled, his eyes misting over, as he beheld her. She kissed him shyly on the cheek, then joined her aunt in the carriage.

The journey to Crattsmore took nearly an hour as they wended their way through West Redditch and into the country on the other side. The sun had set before they got there, but Sarah stared out the window at all the torches lit along the drive up to the great house. It seemed to take forever and her heart kept beating faster as they neared the front steps.

Her aunt was helped out first, and then she emerged from the carriage to look up and around at everything. All the windows shone with candlelight from within and the house fairly glowed in the evening. She lingered a couple steps behind her aunt as they traversed up the path to the front steps.

The Duke of Rothsmere and his family waited at the entrance, greeting guests and Sarah's heart sped up even more as they approached them. But then it was over, before it had even begun. She was welcomed, smiled upon, and then passed down to be free to follow her aunt deeper into the manor after handing their capes off to a servant.

People were everywhere, sometimes clustered so tightly she could hardly move. Her aunt tottered at one point, and she reached forward to grip her arm and steady her. After that she held on, not just to support her, but to keep from being separated in the crush.

Her aunt found a seat and gratefully lowered herself into it, with Sarah standing nearby staring about. A few feet away stood a group of three or four young ladies who appeared to be eyeing her. She smiled in their direction, only to see them exchange glances and turn away.

A look at her aunt told her that she had seen it. Her lined lips pursed and her hand reached up to grip Sarah's for a moment.

The first dance was called and the floor cleared, only to be replaced with couples lining up. A thrill of excitement went through her when the name of the dance was announced. This was one she knew! At the last minute, a young man approached with Duke Rothsmere.

"Lady Touillart, Miss Sarah Mondragón, The Honorable John Newsham has expressed a desire to be introduced to you." He made the introduction and Mr. Newsham stepped forward and bowed.

"Miss Mondragón, I was wondering if you would join me in this dance?"

Sarah nodded, "Yes, of course. Thank you."

He held out his arm and after a moment, she placed her hand on his. He led her out and they took their places only just in time, for the music started and the lead couple stepped off.

Sarah tried to keep track of the couples around her, her place in the dance, the proper steps, and giving her partner some attention. It was nearly too much for her first time dancing in company. She managed to land her steps properly, but she did not trust herself to look up at Mr. Newsham more than once or twice.

By the time the dance ended, Sarah's chest heaved slightly from the exertion. Mr. Newsham led her back to her aunt and she thanked him, but he did not ask her for another dance. Her aunt pulled her down to her level.

"Well done, my dear. Only, try to look at your partner more. This is how young people get to know one another."

"Yes, Aunt."

She watched from the sidelines as another dance progressed, thankful she had not been asked as it was one she did not know. Feeling thirsty, she bent to ask her aunt, "Do you want some refreshment?"

"No, thank you, dear. Go help yourself."

Sarah squeezed through the throng to the adjoining room where she could get a cup of punch and stand out of the way to sip it. She was about to leave when she noticed Lavinia observing her from across the table.

"Miss Esterhay!" she cried in a voice to be heard over the background babble.

"Miss Mondragón!"

They each worked their way to each other and hugged. Sarah hadn't known how forlorn she felt until she saw a familiar, and friendly, face.

"I did not know you were here," Lavinia said.

"I only found out a week ago."

"It's a terrible crush, isn't it?"

"Yes, have you danced yet?"

"No, you?"

"Once. That was quite enough!"

Lavinia chuckled. "I must return to my mother, but good luck."

"Thank you, you as well."

Sarah found her way back to her aunt, but had only been standing there for a few minutes before she was approached by another young man. Once again she was introduced and asked to dance. With a backward glance at her aunt, she allowed herself to be led to the floor.

This dance was one her dancing master had only just started her on, and she felt a momentary qualm about whether or not she could do it. But it was too late now; the music started and the dancers stepped off.

She watched the other dancers and her own feet. There was no chance to look up at her partner this time as she struggled her way through. Then, it happened.

She stepped to the left, only to careen into her neighbor who was stepping to the right. The force of it knocked both the gentleman and her off balance. Her shoe slipped out from under her, tossing her to the floor where another dancer tripped over her. As dancers moved around them, trying to keep it going despite the disruption, Sarah pushed herself up from the floor and ran.

Shaking, she shoved her way through the people until she came to the foyer where a few servants stood waiting. One stepped forward and she said, "Please, my cloak."

She described it and he went off, just as her aunt appeared from the direction of the ball room. Without saying anything she motioned for her own wrap and asked that their carriage be called. Then she came to stand beside her great-niece. After a short while, the carriage arrived and they headed down the steps to where the footman waited. It wasn't until they were safely in the carriage that her aunt spoke.

"My dear, it was an awful thing to happen. But you mustn't worry over it."

"Aunt, it was disastrous. I caused a scene."

Suddenly, the tears that had been threatening burst forward and Aunt Genevieve dug a handkerchief from her reticule. Sarah clasped it to her eyes and sobbed. Her aunt reached across and patted her back.

"Let it out, and you will feel better."

"I'm so sorry to have disappointed you."

"Nonsense, I was very proud to show you off tonight. But this is all our fault for pushing you too hard."

Sarah dragged in a ragged breath. "No, Aunt, I simply made a mistake. I suppose I should have stayed to face it, but I simply could not."

"I understand…Next time—"

"No. I can't."

"You will. Just give it time."

Sarah simply shook her head.

By the time they arrived back at Wrottlesby, her tears had run their course. They went into the house to find her grandfather still awake.

He frowned at them. "It's early for you to be home."

Her aunt explained and her grandfather's lips pursed. Sarah sat waiting for the admonition she knew was coming, but instead he said, "Never mind, my dear. We should have started you at a few assembly dances and local suppers. Your aunt and I were greedy. We couldn't wait to show you off."

"Grandfather, I think I must go home for a while."

Both of them cried out at the same time but she continued, "I need to go somewhere that I can succeed for a while. I will come back, I just need to see my father and the horses, and…I don't know."

"I do, my dear. When would you like to go?" he asked.

"Tomorrow, if possible."

"Then have your maid pack your things."

"I will leave some here for when I come back."

"You must promise me you will."

"I do. I shall. I promise." She rose and kissed both of them before heading off to her room.

It was nearly noon the next day before the carriage rolled up to the front of the manor to await Sarah and her trunk. She had elected to leave Elsie behind and rely solely upon Emma for help with dressing.

Her grandfather and aunt came to the door with her and she hugged them both.

"Thank you, for everything."

"Come back, my dear," her grandfather said, his eyes suspiciously bright.

"I will."

Then she was in the carriage and it set off.

****

The journey home took three days, and she was weary of the travel. And yet, when they entered the environs of Withcombe, a spark of awareness went through her. Not only would she see her father, but possibly the duke. As the carriage passed by the manor house, she stared at it, wondering what he was doing.

She had not had a chance to send a letter to her father announcing her return, so she hoped it would be a welcome surprise for him. The carriage pulled up to the quadrangle and she stepped out while the driver loosed her trunk. Her father sat in his chair by the stoop, and his eyes narrowed on her for a moment, then widened as his mouth dropped open.

"Sarah? Is it really you?"

"*Aitatxo*, it is me!"

He stood with difficulty and threw his arms around her, then pulled back. "But I am dirty from the stables. I will ruin your fine clothes."

"Oh, *Aitatxo*, never!"

Emma came out, wiping her hands on her apron and cried, "Oh, my goodness! It's her! It's you! You're here!"

Sarah laughed, joy bubbling up within her. She looked around at the circle of stable lads and grooms who had stopped their work to steal a glance at her and she waved at them. She turned to Emma and said, "Oh, I need a bath and a change of clothes. Could you help me with the latter?"

"Yes, of course. Just let me know when you are ready."

Two grooms went past carrying her trunk and Emma went off to show them where to put it. Sarah untied the ribbons of her bonnet and went inside to set it on the table. Arnas followed her.

"What am I going to do with you?"

She smiled. "Same as you always did. I will help Henry with the training and the horses."

"But, you are a fine lady now…"

"I am the daughter of the finest horsemaster in England."

"And the granddaughter of an earl."

"First and always, your daughter, *Aitatxo*."

A commotion drew their attention to the opening of the quad and Sarah saw the duke standing there. He paused, then he came forward until he stood before her.

"I saw a carriage go by and wondered who had come. You're home!"

"Yes, for now."

"You aren't going back are you?"

"I must, after a time."

"Perhaps you would join me for a ride sometime."

Her heart constricted as their gazes stayed locked

on one another's. "Yes," she said. "Of course." Suddenly self-conscious, she ducked her head down and turned to go into the house.

"When?" he asked, reaching forward as though to stop her.

She thought quickly. "Tomorrow? After tea?"

"Yes. Until then."

"Until then."

She followed her father into the cottage and shut the door. Standing still for a moment, she struggled to settle her beating heart and her breathing. Emma bustled about in the kitchen and her father stumped over to his chair and sat with a sigh.

With a grin, she looked around the little cottage and climbed upstairs to her room. Emma followed with a ewer of warm water and helped her out of her dress. She lit a fire in the grate before patting Sarah's cheek and leaving.

Sarah looked around her room as she divested herself of the dress. She went through her trunk until she found one of her old dresses and pulled it out. She fastened up the drop front and tied the sash in place behind her. Her dark apron hung behind her door and she slipped it on. Her old work boots still stood in the corner where she had left them and she stepped into them with a slight grimace. They felt heavy after months of light footwear.

Clomping down the stairs, she waved at Emma and her father before going out into the stable yard. After watching the comings and goings for a moment, she headed for the first stall.

Bard's head appeared as soon as she reached it and he nickered toward her. She hugged his head, then his neck as he raised it.

"I owe you my life, you wonderful boy."

She checked his bedding and his manger, then sneaked him a handful of oats before moving on. Touching each horse that greeted her, she felt ever more like she had come home. When she got to the broodmares' stalls there were only two in use, and the foals had grown and they and their mothers would soon be turned out to the pasture. She patted the two dams before moving on.

When she had finished with the quad, she made her way down to the barn, passing the mares' pastures as she went. In one small paddock that reached up the hill, Blue grazed at its end.

"Blue!" she called.

His head shot up, mane bouncing. He nickered and started trotting towards her.

Leaning on the fence rail, she watched him approach, looking for any signs that he was favoring a leg or stiff in some joint. But he moved freely and well, head bobbing with each step. He shoved his nose at her and she scratched him under his chin and jaw the way he liked. Then she dug in the pocket of her overcoat and pulled out a handful of oats to feed him.

He followed her along the fence as she moved on, then stopped and watched her as she headed toward the barn.

The barn was warmer than the outside, and she met the duke's dapple gray hunter first. He remained with his hindquarters toward her and she moved along. When she had finished with the barn she went to the hayloft and hunted some eggs the chickens had laid. It was the stable boy's duty to find the eggs and bring them to Emma, but she had always loved looking for them and couldn't resist.

With three eggs in her hands, she headed back to the cottage, stopping to add them to the basket under the cooking shed. Emma and Edith were just about to serve supper, so she went into the cottage to get cleaned up.

She and her father sat at the table as Emma brought in a pot of stew. They had smelled it all afternoon, and their stomachs were growling by now.

Emma grinned, tiredly, as she served up the bowls and passed them round. "It's wonderful to have Sarah back. What made you want to come home, dear?"

Sarah poked at a piece of meat and said, "I had a disastrous ball, embarrassing for the earl, my grandfather, and my great-aunt. I suppose I was ashamed, and I just wanted to be home. Somewhere that I would not fail."

"Oh, I'm sure they were not embarrassed...Things happen..."

"No, Emma. I disgraced myself. I will not be invited to other functions, and they worked so hard to make me a lady."

"You should give it another chance," Arnas said.

Sarah's head shot up and she stared at him. "I would have thought you'd want me home."

"I did. I do. But I don't like you running away."

She pushed a parsnip around in her bowl. "I don't think I ran away, so much as needed a change. I needed to be somewhere I could succeed, and do well. All I know is horses."

Emma covered her hand with her own. "No, you know far more than that. It's just you know so much

155

about horses; everything else seems small!"

Sarah smiled and gripped her hand back. "Thank you."

"Speaking of the horses, what did you find on your rounds?"

"All seems well. Boomer is still stiff, but with all this cold that is to be expected. The duke's hunter seems acclimatized, but a bit unsocial."

"Yes, we have been working with him."

"Blue seems happy in pasture."

"I think he likes being next to the mares and their foals."

Sarah chuckled. "I imagine so."

She rose to collect their bowls and spoons and took them outside where dishes were being washed. The scullery maids smiled and waved to her and she grinned back. Then, as she went back inside, she wondered what her grandfather and aunt were doing. A deep longing to see them, to be with them filled her. She went to her father's desk and wrote to them, ending it with love and sealing it with her father's stamp. Then she decided to take the letter to the manor to place with the rest of the post.

Instead of her old overcoat, she pulled on her *pelisse* and changed out of her heavy work boots into her lighter laced ones. Carrying her letter, she headed up the rise to the manor house.

The door opened before she could reach the steps and the duke came out.

"What are you doing here?"

"I have a letter to post."

"I will put it with the others if you like."

"Yes, thank you."

His gaze bored into her and she dropped hers after a moment. He stepped forward and took the letter from her hand, then tipped her face up to his. Before she knew it, he bent down and kissed her.

She leaned into it, opening her mouth to his and feeling the movement of him against her. For a full minute he kissed her before she jerked backward with a gasp.

"Your grace!"

"William."

"I…"

"Say it…"

"William," she whispered.

"Sarah," he said.

The door opened and the butler cleared his throat as they broke apart. "The Marchioness of Lilsbury is calling for you, your grace."

William's eyes rolled and Sarah turned back toward the stables without a word. She stumbled once, then caught herself and hurried on.

Kissed! Like nothing she had ever experienced! Her heart still hammered in her chest, and yet she nearly choked on her own breath. Such a kiss… She did not know how she would bear it.

Without seeing the horses or the stable lads, she made her way through the courtyard to the cottage and up the stairs to her room. Once there she undressed quickly, climbed into her nightdress and into bed. She could not bear the thought of something or someone coming between her and what she had just experienced.

She wanted to lie in bed, with the effects of his kiss still upon her.

Chapter Nineteen

William watched Sarah as she stumbled down the rise toward the stables. His breath came fast, and he could not trust himself to speak. He simply followed Jarvis into the house and went to the sitting room where his mother stood glaring at him.

"What were you thinking? Kissing her in front of everyone?"

"Only those who were prying."

"If I saw, you can trust one or more of the servants did."

He shrugged. "I'm not apologizing for anything—"

"It's a matter of appropriate conduct. Are you going to make a mistress of her? Certainly you will not marry her."

"Why not?"

"Think, William. Think of what happens afterward. Family, children, connections. Will you have her father up here at holidays, then send him back with the horses? *Think*, William!"

"It was you pushing me to marry—"

"There is a perfectly acceptable wife waiting upstairs in her room," she said in a hushed voice. "She is trying for all she is worth to snare you. Let her!"

"Speaking of Maggie, she called for me." He left, his steps heavy and fast. He all but jogged up the stairs away from his mother and toward the marchioness.

His pace slowed as he came to her door. He knocked lightly, hoping it would not be heard, but a maid opened it quickly and stepped back to allow him in.

Maggie lay draped across her bed in *déshabille*. One bare foot peeked out from under the dressing gown in what was intended to be a tantalizing manner. He ignored it.

"You wanted to see me?"

"Oh, William. I feel stronger when you are near. Would you read to me?"

"Of course, what shall I read?"

"I have *The Mysteries of Udolpho* there. The place is marked." She leaned back, slightly exposing the space between her breasts.

He sat in the chair and picked up the book, thumbed to the place and began to read. It was a particularly dark section, which hinted at hidden skeletons and worse.

The marchioness shuddered and reached out to him. "Oh, how can Mrs. Radcliffe imagine these things! Horrid!"

"It is but a story. Do you want me to stop?"

"Yes, please. Talk to me of something pleasant so that I won't have horrid dreams."

He sighed. "If you are feeling better, you can come riding with Miss Mondragón and me tomorrow."

"Miss Mondragón? The horse girl?"

"Yes, I asked her to ride with me, but of course she can't ride alone with me."

She sat up, her face twisted in indignation. "You want me to be a chaperone for the horse girl?"

"No, I put it wrong. I thought you might feel up to

it and wish to ride out with me. She is just home from her grandfather the earl's and so I asked her along."

Maggie's chin lifted. "I shall have to see how I feel in the morning. My head was very weak today."

William rose, "I hope you are better in the morning. Good night."

With a sigh of relief he closed the door behind him and he made his way to his own room. But the gong went off, and he headed down to the dining room for supper. He stood waiting, knowing he wasn't quite appropriately dressed. Sure enough, his mother drew up at the sight of him and turned her head away. He ignored the action.

"Hello, Mother."

"William."

Just then, Maggie appeared from the arched entrance and floated on a gauzy train to her place. "Hello, your grace."

"Maggie, you're up."

"I felt I must make the effort. I've been an inconvenience for far too long."

"Nonsense, child. You have a delicate constitution that must be tended to." The duchess glanced at William.

He said nothing. The first course was served and he ate without really knowing what it was. Soup of some kind, with partridge after? He didn't care. He only wanted Sarah to be seated at his table and to finally take precedence over the women currently present.

"This partridge is wonderful, so full of flavor. Is it from Withcombe?" the marchioness asked.

William nodded. "I expect so. I know the gamekeeper did some shooting last week."

"Do you hunt or shoot or whatever it's called?"

"I did, when I was younger. I have left it off in later years. I suppose it is something I must take up again."

"So cruel, and yet how do we live without it?"

"No more cruel than a wolf when it kills, less so I expect. They fairly tear into their prey, often eating before it is completely dead."

The clinks of two forks being set down echoed in the dining room. William looked up into the horrified expressions of Maggie and his mother.

"William! At the dinner table!"

"What?"

"I can't eat now... Such a horrid thought!" Maggie said.

William rubbed his forehead momentarily and then said, "I apologize, ladies. Shall I discuss the new foals born so far?"

"My card party tomorrow evening. Magdalene, you are welcome of course."

"I thank you, but I am no good at cards. I will keep William company."

William focused instead on his meal and wondering what Sarah was doing. He was suddenly aware that someone was calling his name and he looked up, frowning.

"What?"

Maggie leaned toward him. "Your grace, I was hoping you could tell me the name of a *modiste*. My riding habit was torn when I fell."

"I do not know, but Hinckley probably will. I'll ask her when we are finished with dinner."

"My head is feeling weak all of a sudden. I think I

shall retire."

"Of course. Do you need anything?"

"Perhaps your arm, for support. Though I hate to take you from the table."

"Nonsense. Of course I will help you."

He rose, dabbed his mouth with the napkin, and went to her side with his arm out. She grasped it in both of her hands and leaned upon him. He tried to move quickly, but she seemed determined to go as slowly as possible.

He tried to subdue his impatience, but he truly only wanted to get her to the room and leave her so he would be free for the evening. As they reached the door, she opened it and turned to him, face lifted up as though an offering. He frowned down at her, not quite knowing what was expected of him, and stepped back. Then bowed abruptly and turned on his heel.

"William!"

He paused and looked around.

Her head lay tilted to one side and she said, "Goodnight, my dear. Dream of me…"

"Er…good night. I hope you feel better in the morning." He hurried off before she could reply.

His mother by now was in the sitting room and he sighed, for there was really no escape from it. He sat in his father's old chair beside the fire, trying not to look at his mother sitting in her accustomed chair just across from him.

She sighed. "Someday another woman will sit here with you."

William's mind went to Sarah and wondered what she would be like in the evenings. Would she be checking on horses, going over ledgers and pedigrees, or sitting quietly?

"Not for a while, Mother."

"It should be soon, William."

"As soon as I find someone."

"I had hoped you had already found someone."

"How did you... I mean, no. Not yet."

"Oh, did something happen just now? Nay, nay, I won't intrude. Keep your secrets."

"Mother, nothing happened. Please do not speculate."

She lifted a lined hand and nodded, but a smile played about her lips and William sighed to himself. Now his mother would think him secretly engaged to Maggie, and he didn't know how to disabuse her of the idea.

He picked up a book and opened it to a random page. Though an interesting treatise on the various fungi of southern England, it was unable to hold his attention for long, despite the intricate drawings.

After setting it aside, he stirred the fire with the poker. His mother made a *moue* of distaste, her mouth wrinkling up.

"Oh William, don't. The ashes will get all over."

"Yes, Mother."

Suddenly restless, he rose and said, "I'm going out for a walk. I will see you in the morning."

"Goodnight, then."

A sense of freedom rushed through him. He strode to the foyer and demanded his coat. It was brought and he was helped into it, then he set off into the darkness.

The soles of his shoes slipped a little on the gravel leading off to the stables. His breath condensed into white puffs that wreathed his head as he walked. The ground was dark, hidden from him and he was forced to step more carefully than he would have otherwise.

The lights were on in the cottage and he headed straight for the little stoop. He knocked and waited. He heard her step approaching and a thrill jolted through him. The door opened.

She stood there in her dressing gown, with her hair tumbled all around her face and shoulders. The moonlight peeked out through the cloud cover for a moment to reflect itself in her eyes. He bent to kiss her but her hand shot up and she turned her head.

"Your grace, please don't."

"But Sarah, I love you."

"You can't. You mustn't."

A stumping sounded from behind her and she fled. He was left to stare at Arnas.

The older man lifted a hand to him. "Let her go, your grace. Do not meddle with my daughter. She is all I have, and she is so young."

"I'm not meddling."

"What are your intentions?"

"I don't know… I have hopes…"

"Hopes? You hold our lives in your hand and you speak of hopes? The old duke would not have acted this way."

"What way?"

"Seducing my daughter beyond her reason and ability to say no. She is conflicted and confused, and you are not thinking."

Rage roiled through him suddenly. "Careful, old man."

"Oh, I know. You could kick us out of here, throw us beyond the gates. Possible you could live with yourself, too. Do you know what made your father great? He respected those who toiled beneath him. He understood the give and take between servant and master."

"As do I!"

"Then leave my daughter alone!"

"I cannot. I love her, and she feels the same for me; I am certain."

"But she has had no one to compare. You are the first man to come along and who else does she have? How does she even know how she feels?"

"You seduced the daughter of an earl once."

"And I know of what I speak. My wife regretted her actions. Love is not always enough. I know, if it were possible to have fixed my wife's heart with love alone, it would have been done. Had I restrained myself and left her alone, she might be alive today."

His words hit a chord deep within William and he stepped back. "What would you have me do?"

"Let her go. Leave her alone and let her live in her world, perhaps find a boy in our world. Perhaps she will find her feelings for you are not what she thinks. Maybe they are, but then she will know."

William stared at the once powerful man. Arnas's eyes glittered in the moonlight. Finally, William nodded. Without speaking he walked away and the door behind him closed. He paused for a moment, struggling with the emotions whirling through him, urging him to turn around and claim the woman he loved. But then...

He continued walking.

Chapter Twenty

Sarah stood in the kitchen, listening to her father yelling at the duke. What would he do? Sudden fear shot through her. What if he threw them out, what would they do? Would the earl take them in? Could her father find another place? But surely, the duke would not retaliate like that…

Would he?

She waited for his response, but there was none. Just the door closing and her father's limp coming toward her. And then, the meaning of her father's words hit her. Her mother had regretted…

"You heard?"

She nodded her head. "Is it true? My mother…"

"She found that the reality of our life exceeded her love for me. Never for you. She loved you with all her heart. I think, though, she had given up on life long before the sickness took her. I do not want the same for you."

"But surely, it would be different for me."

"Sarah, why did you come home from the earl's house?"

"I…I found I did not belong."

"And you had a choice, to come back here. If you marry the duke, you will not have that choice. There will be no getting away from him."

She stared at the floor, shadowed from the single

candle that flickered beside her hand. "Father, I must face this. I must go back to my grandfather's and face this."

"Yes, my dear. No more running."

"No. No more."

****

It was early when Bard and Roger were hitched to the cart and Sarah's trunk stowed safely in the back. Henry helped her up onto the seat and she waved listlessly to her father as the horses started off. She forced herself not to look up at the manor as they passed by. Instead she focused on Bard, the bunching and relaxing of his muscles as he pulled his share of the weight. Then her gaze drifted to the road, and then the town in the distance.

Three days later, Wrottlesby rose from the low hills as they crested the last rise. For some reason, she felt like she wanted to cry, but instead she sniffed hard and forced a smile. As she was helped down from the seat of the wagon, the door to Wrottlesby opened.

Her aunt was the first to greet her, enveloping her in wraithlike arms. Then her grandfather stepped forward, took her hands and blinked back tears.

"Oh, my dear, let's get you a warm bath and some fresh clothes. I know you will feel better. Don't worry about dressing for supper. I will have a tray sent up to you. Elsie! A bath for Miss Mondragón."

"Yes, ma'am. Oh, miss, it is so good to see you!"

"Bath, Elsie."

Elsie bobbed again and scuttled off. Her grandfather turned to her.

"Your room is just as you left it. We are expecting my cousin and her sons in a couple of days. You will have some young people to talk to!"

The thought made Sarah's heartbeat wane momentarily. She forced a smile, and hugged them once more before heading up the stairs to her room.

Elsie was busy bringing cans of heated water up from the kitchen to pour into the tub. She helped Sarah undress and sink into the delightfully warm water. She leaned back against the tub and sighed.

The water cooled, so she quickly washed up and stepped into the towel Elsie held up. She dried quickly in front of the fire, then dressed in her nightgown and dressing gown. By then, the promised tray had arrived.

By the time Sarah climbed into bed, she was warm and clean and full. A sense of satisfaction warred with the sorrow of being away from Withcombe, her father, and the duke.

William. She closed her eyes. His last kiss had been hungry; it had awakened feelings long dormant but now they clamored for fulfillment. And yet, could they not be together? She knew the daughter of a horseman and the son of a duke did not belong together, and yet they did. Somehow, they had to find a way...

She slept, and did not waken until morning was long underway. Elsie bumped the wall with the tray. She startled awake.

"Sorry!" her maid whispered.

She pushed a stray tendril of hair from her face and sighed. "Mmmph, I slept too long."

"Mayhap you needed it, miss."

"What is that you've brought me?"

"Eggs, toast, and tea. And strawberry jam."

"Sounds lovely."

She moved back to allow Elsie to set the tray over

her lap and then poured some tea. It was hot and strong, just as she liked it. She set the cup down and leaned back, watching Elsie moving through the room, replacing the clothes she had cleaned and pulling out a new morning dress for Sarah to wear.

When she was dressed and her hair done to Elsie's satisfaction, she went downstairs in search of her aunt and grandfather. Morning light slanted in through the windows as the clock in the hallway sounded ten o'clock.

She found them in the parlor, her grandfather smoking a pipe and her great-aunt was embroidering. They both looked up as she entered and smiled.

"Ah, there you are, my dear. Looking lovely as ever!" the earl said.

"How long since you practiced your piano?"

Sarah bit her lip and Genevieve pointed to the pianoforte in the corner. Sarah went through some warm-ups before practicing a couple of simple songs. The earl and his sister listened with complacent expressions, and she practiced until her hands could do no more.

She went to the fireplace to warm her fingers for a moment before sitting down. He grandfather gestured about with his pipe.

"As I said last night, my cousin Marie de la Fontaine is coming with her two sons. She is married to the Duke of Ellenston, but she lives at the country estate in Surrey. Her sons are Wendell, Lord Farnham and Lord Peter."

"Lord Farnham and Lord Peter. All right."

"And, 'your grace,'" Genevieve said.

"Whew! How long will they be here?"

"A week. The boys are great hunters, so I thought we'd have a hunt while they are here. I've got the hounds scheduled for Friday."

"And I thought we would have another supper party with some of the local young men and women."

"No dancing."

"No, dear. No dancing. Some of the girls will play, no doubt, but your job will simply be to talk and look beautiful."

"Well, I can talk at least…"

"No false modesty, my dear."

The day passed quietly, a relief to Sarah after the rigors of travel. She sat on the settee by the window and let the sunshine play over her. Falling asleep in the warmth of the light coming in through the window and waking up in time for tea, yet still thinking about the duke's kiss. Nothing seemed able to shake that memory from her consciousness. It was always there, ready to seduce her attention from whatever else may be going on.

The cousins arrived in the afternoon of the following day. The carriage's polished surface shone and the horses matched its deep ebony color. Sarah stood with her aunt and grandfather to welcome them to Wrottlesby.

The duchess stepped out first. Her *pelisse* seemed to have come straight from France. Her golden hair may have had some silver mixed in, but it was beautifully arranged. Her sons were around Sarah's age, Peter a little younger, while Wendell was slightly older. Both were dressed handsomely, and Sarah would have sworn their outfits were chosen to set off the duchess's.

The duchess swept down and greeted the earl and

Lady Touillart sweetly, but hesitated before pronouncing Sarah's name.

The tips of his mustache pointed up as the earl introduced Sarah. "My granddaughter, Miss Mondragón."

The duchess pasted a half-smile on her face as Sarah curtseyed. Peter gave her half a bow, but Wendell ignored her completely and walked past into the house, leaving her confused. Her aunt touched her shoulder as they followed their guests into the manor and Sarah took some comfort in that.

They all congregated in the parlor where tea was ordered. The boys descended upon the crispy tarts and macaroons as though they had not eaten in days while Sarah sat silently with her cup and saucer. She had been served last, and for some reason that hurt. She understood precedence well enough, but the fact that Peter would be served before her galled.

She took a bite of her crispy tart and listened to the duchess expound on their journey.

"Really, Edmund, if you had seen what they put us in, you would have pitied me. The only room they had left was a double bed meant to share. I immediately booked both sides as I was not about to have some lice-ridden peasant crawl into bed with me in the middle of the night. It's all right for the boys; they can share, but really!"

"Well, well, no harm done!"

"I am so looking forward to a real supper tonight! We've had nothing but tavern offerings for days."

Genevieve leaned forward. "We are having veal tonight."

"Oh, lovely! Wendell, play that song you have

been practicing on the Broadwood Grand at home."

"Mother…" he whined.

"Come now. Play."

Wendell went to the piano and played a very sloppy rendition of a waltz, then slouched away before his mother could entice him to play again.

"Sarah," said her grandfather, "Play that song you were playing earlier."

Panic shot through her, and she wanted to shake her head and flee, but she had promised her father not to run away any more. So she rose and went to the piano, arranged her music, and played the little Irish tune.

Wendell humphed. "I played that when I was eight."

The earl looked benignly at him. "I'll wager you did not play it anywhere like that."

Wendell rolled his eyes but said nothing.

"And then there's Peter, my equestrian."

"I am glad we brought Flash with us."

"Your father thought the journey too long, but we prevailed."

"He's fine, fit and sound."

"We are having a hunt in a couple of days," the earl said.

"Oh, I say, that will be fun," Peter said.

Wendell stood abruptly. "I'm going to the library. Which way is it again?"

The earl gestured out toward the hall and said, "Down the hall, to your right. Can't miss it."

Without thanking the earl, he headed off. Peter stood as well.

"I'm going to go check on Flash, if that's all right."

"Yes, of course. Sarah, perhaps you will show Lord Peter to the stables."

"Yes, Grandfather." Sarah said.

Peter opened his mouth as though to protest. Sarah rose, collected her *pelisse*, and led the way toward the stables. They went out through the kitchen, pausing by the basket of vegetables to each grab a carrot before heading out the servants' entrance towards the low-roofed stables.

Built of stone and wood, the buildings seemed destined to last indefinitely. Sarah strode through the double-doored entry into the breezeway where two horses were being groomed. Stopping by Arthur, Sarah fed him pieces of the carrot, while Peter continued on until he found his horse, Flash. True to his name, he was a shining, light chestnut, tall and lean, though with large thighs for jumping. Peter fed part of his carrot to Flash, and then the rest to the horse stabled beside him.

"This is Endeavor, Wendell's horse. Not that he ever does much with him. And he is a magnificent thing. Father brought him back from Spain for Wendell."

"My father is from Spain. Well, Basque country, but Spain."

"I say, does he speak Spanish?"

"And Basque. In fact, his English was rather poor until my mother helped him. Now you would hardly know, except he still has something of an accent."

"Do you speak Basque?"

"A few words. Most of them are not supposed to be spoken by a lady."

"Oh, you must tell me one."

She glanced around, then whispered, "*Arraoia*."

"*Arraoia*. What does it mean?"

"I don't know what it means in English," she said, though she knew perfectly well.

"Do you like to ride?"

"More than anything."

"Let's go riding tomorrow. Maybe we can convince old Wendell to leave the books behind and go with us."

In the end, it was just the two of them riding the next day, with a groom following. Sarah was happy to see that Lord Peter knew how to handle his horse well, and the two of them chased rabbits, jumped hedgerows, and galloped freely across the fields. It was the first time Sarah had an equal to ride with, and she found it exhilarating, making her wonder what the duke was like on horseback.

They wandered sedately along, giving the horses a rest, and she imagined him astride Bard, or one of the other Withcombe horses. She could only think how fine he would look.

"I say, this is fun. I never have anyone to ride with at home. Mummy won't let Wendell risk himself. Luckily, no one really cares what I do."

"Surely that's not true!" Sarah cried.

He sighed. "It's true. She even calls me the 'spare.' Wendell is the 'heir.' Doesn't really matter what I do, as long as they have Wen."

"Well, if you measure people like that, then I suppose I am completely worthless. I am the daughter of a horsemaster, granddaughter to an earl. Really, I'm nobody."

"You're a cracking good equestrienne. Can't wait to see you on the hunt."

She smiled. "I'm looking forward to it. It will be my first."

The sun had lowered to the horizon by the time they returned to the manor house. The gong rang as Sarah was changing out of her riding habit and Elsie's lips pursed.

"Eh, miss, you need to hurry."

"Never mind my hair. Just do up the back and I'll slip on the shoes."

As soon as Elsie finished, Sarah shot out of the room and made it to the dining room as the last bell rang. Blowing out a breath of relief, she sat down, smiling at Peter who caught her eye and grinned.

"And did you enjoy your ride, my sweet?" the duchess asked her son.

He nodded, mouth full of soup which he swallowed and said, "Sarah is an excellent rider, Mummy. You should have come out and watched us race."

"Peter, the sun and wind are quite awful for the complexion. I'm surprised Sarah risked it. She will grow quite brown and coarse."

"I can't imagine Sarah looking anything except fresh and beautiful," her grandfather said.

Sarah smiled down into her bowl.

The duchess was silent, then said, "Wendell, did you discover anything new in your search?"

"I found a painting of the fourth Duke of Ellenston. I say painting; it is no more than a miniature but quite well done."

"Is that not serendipitous! Visiting family is always fun like that." She smiled upon her eldest son who sat beside Sarah and her gaze happened to fall upon her. The duchess's expression turned stony, and she looked away.

Sarah's back stiffened and she set her spoon down to await the next course. The duchess's disparagements were becoming commonplace to her. She understood the source; the woman obviously felt her to be beneath them. But she had been kissed by a duke. Even though she knew he was conflicted about her, that one fact stiffened her resolve and helped her to ignore the constant slights.

Her grandfather's mouth compressed under his mustache and he was silent for a moment, then he said, "We thought about having a small dance next week. Do you boys like to dance?"

Wendell sniffed. "If there are any partners worth the effort."

"Oh, I think we can find you partners enough. We have a broad acquaintance."

"I say, that sounds splendid. Sarah, will you dance with me?" Peter smiled from across the table.

"I'm sure Sarah will have plenty of boys of suitable caliber vying to dance with her," the duchess said rather quickly.

Sarah turned to Peter. "I would be happy to partner with you, Lord Peter, and leave you to choose the dance."

She delighted in seeing the way the duchess's chest heaved in displeasure.

Chapter Twenty-One

William sat in the darkness of the parlor. The candles had burned down, and he relished the shadows for the time being. He craved the darkness, for it mirrored his heart at the moment.

He was in love with Sarah; that fact was obvious to him. His soul burned for her, and he could barely contain himself from marching down to the stables and carrying her off. But the rational side of him held firm, and he remained where he was, simply longing for a life that seemed denied him.

The old horsemaster's words had hit home. Sarah's mother had regretted her choice. Would Sarah one day come to feel the same? How many snubs and cold shoulders could one person take?

How much could he take?

He did not know. Could he divorce himself from society to the degree that would be necessary? Would his own love one day falter under the weight of societal deprivation? He didn't think so. At any rate he could not imagine feeling this way for anyone else. He covered his face with one hand and sighed.

The servant came in ."Oh, your grace, I did not know you were here or I would have lit the candles sooner."

"No matter." Ellen or Helen? "I am leaving now."

His room was cold, the fire only just beginning to

take the chill off the air. He stripped and pulled on a nightshirt before falling into bed. Pinching out the candle on the nightstand, he stared once more into the darkness. Somewhere, down the low hill, Sarah was in bed as well. Was she thinking about him? Did she long for him the way he craved after her?

Blessed sleep came, bringing dreams where he sought for something that he could not find, and ran in slow motion away from a danger he could not see. When the curtains were opened the next morning, the light found him wide awake.

After breakfast, he determined to ride. He would invite Sarah to join him and let her decide. If she wanted him to court her, then her decision would let him know. For himself, he was sure., It was now up to her.

He left the house without eating breakfast and strode over the slick, frost-ridden grass toward the stables. Once there, he went straight to the cottage and knocked on the door. A bustling step, and then it was opened by Emma. Her eyes widened and she dropped a curtsey,

"Duke Tensington."

"Can you inform Miss Mondragón that I am here?"

"I'm sorry your grace, but I cannot. She is gone."

"What? Here, Mondragón!" he called and peered around Emma's compact bulk.

The sound of Arnas's stumping walk sounded and he came around the corner.

"Your grace?"

"Where is Sarah?"

"She has gone to her grandfather."

"She was sent, you mean."

"She went of her own volition. This was her decision."

"When?"

"Just this morning…"

"Saddle my horse."

Arnas hesitated a moment, then edged around the duke to the stoop and called to a nearby groom. "Bring the duke's horse. Make sure he is saddled and ready."

The boy shot a terrified look to the duke and scuttled off. It took nearly half an hour for the horse to be delivered. William climbed aloft, not caring whether he did so well or not, and tried to remember Sarah's lesson on balance. He paused for a moment to find that spot, then urged the horse forward.

He broke into a heavy jog that bounced William uncomfortably so he pushed the horse into a slow canter and fell quickly into the rhythm of it. The ground rushing by still caused his heart to beat faster, but so did the thought of getting Sarah back. She could not be far ahead of him.

They cantered along the gravel road toward the town, rising up the side of the hill that overlooked it. When he had reached the top, he paused to look down the road and see if he could see the cart.

And there it was, about to disappear into the town.

He started to urge the horse forward and stopped. The cart neared the main thoroughfare to the town and disappeared inside.

He let her go.

He could not explain the thoughts that went through his brain, save the fact that Arnas would deny his daughter nothing, and that meant she had truly chosen to leave. The idea may have been Mondragón's, but she had been willing.

Slowly, he turned the horse around. Sensing a return to rest and food, the horse's pace picked up and he once again broke into the uncomfortable trot. William pulled back on the reins and the horse stopped. He made to move his boot, but it stuck in the stirrup so he reached down to free it. His heel collided soundly with the horse's flank.

The horse jumped, hopped violently once or twice, then bolted while William was still bent over his boot. All balance gone, he tried to hang on, but the horse veered toward the trees. William's face struck one of the trees, pulling him off the horse and tossing him roughly to the ground.

The world went dark.

Chapter Twenty-Two

Wearing her twilight blue riding habit, Sarah sat on Arthur. The Master of the Foxhounds sat in his red coat on his own horse near the hounds that milled about their handlers. Horses and riders were everywhere. The thought of all these animals chasing in a group after a single fox frightened Sarah. There was so much that could go wrong…

Peter pulled up next to her on Flash and grinned. "This will be fun, don't you think?"

"Not if someone gets hurt," she said.

He laughed. "That would just make it more exciting!"

She glanced over at Wendell on Endeavor and endured a stab of irritation. His back was slouched, his hands slack with the reins, and he appeared completely disinterested in what was happening around him. And the horse was truly magnificent…Such a waste.

She looked down at her grandfather. "You be careful. Don't attempt anything you can't do."

"I won't, Grandfather. Don't worry."

Peter chuckled again. "I can't imagine anything Sarah can't do!"

The hounds suddenly bayed and a horn blew as the riders took off after the red coated master. Sarah tried to stay near Peter who urged his horse to the head of the pack. A flea-bitten gray horse bumbled in front of her and she was forced to pull up slightly and maneuver around it.

The hounds picked up speed, and she urged Arthur to keep up with the rest. Peter was lost to her, though Wendell was still visible, struggling with his reins and confusing his horse.

They thundered down a low hill and jumped over a stream, charging up the next rise after the hounds. The horn thrilled her each time it blew, as did the shouts of the whippers-in ahead.

The riders ahead of her accelerated and she nudged Arthur to greater speed and prepared to jump the coming hedge. Arthur's muscles bunched underneath her and he sailed easily over, landing soundly on the other side. A flurry of commotion to one side and she looked in time to see Wendell go down in a tangle of legs with his horse.

They were gone, swept along with the pack and racing along a field. Sheep scattered as they surged through the green.

The baying grew more intense, and the horn blew again. Arthur's ears were up, swiveling back to her as she adjusted the reins to take him to the outside of the pack. One there, she raced around the side toward the front where she could see. She caught Peter's eye and he glanced over long enough to grin hugely at her.

The dogs slowed suddenly, milling about sniffing, then surged off in another direction, baying. Sarah did not need to urge Arthur twice. He liked being in the front and pounded forward to stay there.

She and Peter raced neck and neck toward the coming fence. Both horses met it easily, though Flash was clearly tiring. The baying intensified and they pushed their horses again.

Arthur was blowing his breath now and still the hounds bayed.

The riders charged up the next hill toward the copse of trees at the top. Sarah pulled up beside the grove, which was suddenly filled with hounds howling with excitement. Flash stopped beside her and Peter looked over.

"Still on, I see!"

"Isn't everyone?" She panted.

He shook his head. "Wendell went down right away. Hope he's all right. A couple more were lost on the last fence."

"I didn't see anything except the red coats and the hounds. Well, and Wendell going down."

"He probably did it on purpose so he wouldn't have to sit the hunt. Endeavor is wasted on him." He blew out an irritated breath.

"What do we do now?"

"The master is coming your way. I think your grandfather told him this is your first hunt."

Sure enough, the master reached over to wipe his thumb on her forehead, grinning widely at her. She reached up to touch the sticky spot, and her hand came away bloody.

"It's called 'blooding' when they mark you with the blood of the fox," Peter said.

"Has it happened to you?"

"Gosh, yes, ages ago. I can't believe you ride the way you do and yet have never hunted."

"My circumstances are unique."

They were heading back toward the estate now, letting their horses rest with a slow jog.

"Ah yes," he said. "Mother said something about a father who grooms or some such."

"He trains the horses."

"So that's where you get it. Good on you!"

"You don't mind?"

"No, of course not. Wendell probably does, though. Just ignore him. And Mummy."

"I do, for the most part." She sighed, and added, "Lord, I'm hungry."

"Me too. Hopefully they have a good tea laid on for us when we get back."

"Knowing Aunt Genevieve, they do."

Sarah slid to the ground once they reached the manor house at Wrottlesby. A groom stepped up to take Arthur from her and she headed into the house with Peter in tow. Her grandfather stood at the top of the stairs, and he beamed when he caught sight of the mark on her forehead.

"Well, then, first hunt successful!"

"Yes, sir. It was exciting."

"Well, come in; we have a little luncheon ready for you."

Sarah went gratefully to the table set with plates of jellies, cold meats, and salads. Peter sat beside her and ate large helpings of everything. Wendell and his mother were nowhere to be seen. When she had eaten her fill, Sarah went in search of her aunt, finally finding her in the parlor in conversation with Peter's mother.

"And so, he fell. But was aware enough to maneuver out of the way of the other horses, else he would be even more injured."

"Is Lord Farnham all right?" she asked.

"He has a very weak head right now, and his knee

is badly bruised, but he should be well in a couple of days according to the physician," the duchess said. Her eyes widened at Sarah's forehead and she added with a *moue* of disgust, "Horrid tradition. Thank goodness it is dying out."

Sarah's hand went to her forehead and she bit her lip. "Oh yes, let me go wash this off. Excuse me, please."

Elsie met her at her room and offered to help her into one of her afternoon dresses, which Sarah accepted, after sighing. She went first to the basin and poured water from the ewer to wash her face. Then she stood in the center of the room and let Elsie undress and then dress her again, exhaustion finally replacing the adrenaline from the hunt.

By the time she made her way back downstairs, most of the hunters had gone and the servants were putting things back to normal. She wandered about, not sure what she was looking for and ended by the front window, staring at the carriages leaving with horses in tow behind. What would the duke have thought of her performance? Would he have joined in the hunt?

Sorrow filled the space where excitement had been. The hunt had been a welcome respite from her depression, but it could not last. Eventually, she would be left alone with her feelings.

Was this love, this pain that went with the longing to see him again? She did not know what to call it, but she suspected this was love.

She was in love with the duke, and she did not know what to do.

She jumped at a sound behind her and spun around, only to see Peter standing there.

Her hand went to her chest which heaved now, and she said a little sharply, "Lord Peter! You are silent as a ghost!"

"I am so sorry. I did not want to intrude and didn't know how to make myself known. Please forgive me."

"No forgiveness necessary. You simply caught me thinking of home."

"A little homesick?"

She sighed. "You could say that. How is your brother?"

He rolled his eyes. "Oh, living it up. Anything for attention."

"But that was a terrible fall he took."

"You know, I suspect he did it on purpose to get out of hunting."

Her mouth dropped open. "Oh surely not! Such a risk!"

He shrugged and stood beside her. "Never mind. I'm just a little jaded when it comes to my brother."

"I have no brother or sister, and always wished for one."

"I always wished to be the only child." He cleared his throat and said in a different voice, "I say, Miss Mondragón, we are pretty compatible."

"Yes, Lord Peter. I think of us as good friends."

"We could be more than that." He looked at her.

"Oh, sir, I cannot think of anything like that. I…I care about someone else."

He blew out a breath suddenly, and grinned. "Well, that's a relief. I thought we had been set up to make a match of it. I like you awfully, you know, but I don't want to think of anything long lasting right now."

She looked up through her lashes. "So you aren't

angry?"

"No! We can go on as we are, just great friends. Though, I would hope if ever I can be of service, you will let me know."

"Oh, sir, I will. Thank you."

He sketched a little bow, then grinned at her and walked away.

Sarah was oddly touched, but that moment of panic and revulsion at the thought of marrying Lord Peter told her much about her own feelings. What would she do if the duke did not want her?

A servant came in to light the candles and she went to the piano to practice her little song. She found that the piano was becoming something she could not live without. For so long her life had consisted only of horses, and now there were other things vying for her attention. She wasn't sure how she felt about that, but she thought it was a good thing.

The gong rang, and she realized she had sat for too long. She jumped up and ran for the staircase, racing up as quickly as she could while holding her skirt to one side. Elsie was ready for her and unfastened her dress, then helped her slip it off for an evening gown. Sarah dug out her mother's pearls and Elsie secured them around her neck, then patted her hair into place and sent her off.

Her grandfather was tired, but happy, the tips of his mustache pointing upward and his eyes crinkled. She noted that he did not eat much and frowned a little at this. Her aunt gave a little shake of her head and then turned back to the duchess who was talking.

"And so, brave boy, he insisted on coming down for supper, thinking it was his duty. But I prevailed upon him to stay in bed. I had a tray sent up and have since heard he had a good appetite. The physician, I know, was not quite happy about his head but said he would check again in the morning."

"I am glad to hear he is doing better. He looked so pale when he was brought in," Aunt Genevieve said.

"It was the shock. Shock, I am told, can silence the stoutest heart."

"Well, he seems all right now," said Peter.

The duchess frowned in her son's direction and took a bite of squab.

Sarah sighed to herself and wondered how long the duchess and her sons would be staying.

Aunt Genevieve cleared her throat."I have arranged for our little supper and dance to be held three nights hence. Do you think Lord Farnham will be well by then?"

"We will hope so. I know he is pushing himself to be well, and that alone may sabotage nature's course. I will encourage him again to be patient."

Peter jogged Sarah's elbow. "Don't forget you promised to dance with me. Though I must warn you, I'm a rotten dancer."

She chuckled. "Well, we will be well-matched then!"

The duchess frowned and took a sip of wine.

Chapter Twenty-Three

William awoke to a world of pain. His arm lay immobilized beside him, throbbing at the shoulder and his left leg ached from hip to toes. But it was his face and head that gave him the most pain. He tried to open his eyes, only to find that one was swollen shut. He lifted his good hand and felt gingerly about. His nose and eyes were puffy and he wondered what he looked like. He glanced over and with his one good eye saw his valet over by his desk and said in a hoarse voice,

"Larkin, bring me a mirror."

Larkin jumped and spun around, hand at his throat. "Oh, sir, you gave me a fright! I must tell your mother you are awake."

"A mirror first."

Reluctantly, his valet brought the mirror and placed it in William's good hand. He lifted it painfully, but hardly recognized the black and blue mess that was his face.

"Good God! What happened?"

"Don't you remember, sir?"

"No."

"You were smashed against a tree and fell off your horse."

He groaned. What a poor showing! He was grateful Sarah wasn't there to see it. He pushed himself up with his good arm and Larkin rushed to arrange his pillows so he could sit up.

"I must go call your mother and the doctor. Excuse me."

William nodded, but that simple act radiating pain through his face and head. He leaned back and closed his eye. Moments later sounds of a commotion echoed in the hallway and his hand was suddenly taken and pressed against a damp surface.

"William! Oh my son! Alive!"

"Yes, Mother. I am well. Enough, at least."

"Yet you lay as though dead or dying since yesterday."

"It was a nasty blow, I'm told."

"Yes, we are blessed to have you still. I have sent for the doctor. I hope he arrives forthwith."

"What exactly is wrong with me?"

"Oh, I can't remember the details. Something about a shoulder location and a bruised hip or some such. And your face…"

"It will all heal, Mother. Not to worry."

"Oh, but when you were brought in—I thought you were dead. The doctor thought so too, I know he did."

"Well, I am not. I would like some tea and maybe some toast."

She reached over and pulled the bell. They waited in silence until the servant came.

"Fetch some tea and toast for his grace at once."

"Yes, ma'am."

The doctor arrived by the time William had finished his tea. He unbound William's arm and tested its soundness.

"Does that hurt?" he asked as he lifted the arm up and rotated it slightly.

"It is sore, but bearable."

"Excellent. You should thank your stars you were unconscious when I put it back into place. Let's see that hip. Bruise has spread, but luckily I don't think anything is broken or permanently injured. Now, your face…"

Points of pain erupted all over his cheeks and nose as the doctor's hands probed deftly about.

"I wouldn't be surprised if these bones had cracked—that was a nasty hit. But I don't think anything lasting is damaged. In time, the swelling and bruising will go down and you will be your old handsome self."

"And my brain?"

"That has me worried, I confess. We can never be sure how the brain responds to injuries such as yours. We shall have to wait and see, I'm afraid."

"I feel fine, just a little dizzy from time to time."

"Well, rest is what I prescribe. Rest and cool compresses to your face."

"What about meals?"

"Start light, toast, broth, and the like. I'll speak with the kitchen on my way out."

William grumbled at that, but thanked him and leaned back with a groan. His mother bustled back in and hovered like a bee about to land on a flower.

"Please sit, Mother, or go elsewhere."

The chair groaned as she sat, then she reached for his hand. He gently pulled it back, but patted her hands as he did so.

"I am really all right. I'm sorry I look such a mess. Doctor says it will all go down and fade in time."

"I must say I don't think much of that Maggie

person you had here."

"She is a marchioness. Why, what did she do?"

"Took one look at you, screamed, and packed her things to leave. She's gone."

"Well, good riddance I say."

"She would have been a good match for you."

"All she was interested in was money and appearances. I find I want more in a wife."

She pursed her lips; her back straightened; but she said nothing for a moment. "Would you like me to read to you?"

He sighed. "Actually, could you have the steward come see me?"

"Rafferty? Whatever for?"

"To discuss the running of Withcombe."

She took a moment to call a servant to fetch the steward, then looked back at William.

"I'll need to talk to Mondragón, as well. But he won't be able to make it up here so I shall have to go to him."

"Nonsense, you aren't going anywhere!"

"Not today, I grant you. But in a day or so I shall be well enough to go."

"I don't see why he couldn't come to you. That is what servants do."

"He is not just some servant, and he is crippled."

"Then perhaps it is time you found a new horsemaster."

William was silent for a moment. Then he said in a low voice, "Arnas Mondragón will always be horsemaster at Withcombe."

His mother sniffed and looked away.

****

William stood awkwardly in the foyer, leaning on one of his father's canes. The carriage came around and he felt ridiculous calling the carriage to take him to his own stables. But his mother had overridden the cart, and he could not walk so far with his bruised and battered leg…so a carriage it was.

When he sat down on the padded seat, however, he was thankful the carriage had been an option. The bare wood seat of the cart would have been torture on his hip.

The carriage pulled up beside the cottage. William got out and struggled up the steps to knock on the door. It was opened by Emma, who instantly smoothed her apron and patted a loose lock of hair back when she saw him.

"Duke Tensington. Are you here for Arnas?"

"Yes, is he available?"

"I will call him," she said with another glance at his face as William entered and sat at the table.

The dizziness hit him momentarily and he held his head still until it passed. Soon he heard the stumping approach of Arnas Mondragón. The stumping stopped when Arnas caught sight of him, then slowly continued until he, too, was sitting at the table.

"I had heard you were injured, your grace. Are you truly well enough to be here? I would have come to you."

"I am well enough for this, Arnas. I have spoken with Rafferty, who tells me the farms did not produce as much hay and oats as we normally need for the horses. Were you aware of this?"

"Yes, your grace. Usually we purchase more from the local farms."

"But apparently there is not enough income from the rents to support this, unless I borrow against the estate, which I am not willing to do. Father did so, and I must find a way to pay off the note, and support the horses and the estate. I need to find someplace to cut. How many horses could we sell?"

Arnas thought, and William was happy to see that he did not seem angry at his request.

"We have three four-year-olds that are ready, a few three-year-olds, and some two-year-olds coming up. I want to keep one or two of them back for breeding, but say we reduce the herd by ten…Would that help?"

"I am assuming that Rafferty has told you what we have available from the farms. Will that be adequate for the horses until spring?"

Arnas considered, then grabbed a pencil and a scrap of paper to write some figures. He looked up, "We need to cut five more horses. There are two older cart horses that can go to one of the farms. We can use the bays to pull—they are bred for it. If you would be willing to give up your gray, you can use Bard who is a superior horse. Then I will send a couple more out to pasture and we should be good. Remember, too, that we will need fewer stablehands with fewer horses. That would be more savings."

"What will the boys do if let go from here?"

"They will have to find work elsewhere."

William thought for a moment. "I hate to send anyone off with no work."

"We can send them with a month's wages if you like. That will give them time to find new work. All this won't happen overnight, anyway. They will have warning."

William tapped the table. "Excellent. I will leave it with you. Yes, sell the gray. The money we make from these sales may help pay off my father's note." He reached across to shake Arnas's hand and the older man clasped his tightly.

"When things are better, we can increase the herd. This is just temporary."

Arnas nodded and he turned to leave.

William leaned back against the seat with a sigh. He had pushed himself too far and looked forward to his bed and getting of the restrictive clothes that put pressure on all of his sore spots. As the carriage rolled up the rise to the manor, he was grateful not to have to be walking up the whole way.

His mother fluttered about as he came in and he had to kindly, but firmly, send her off. Larkin and the butler helped him up the stairs to his room where his valet helped get him out of his suit and into a loose nightshirt.

Business was done. Now there was nothing to think about except Sarah. What was she doing? Had she met someone? Had she forgotten him? He remembered their kiss, and the way her body had melded against his for that one sacred moment.

No, she can't have forgotten that…

His mother came in, followed by a maid carrying a tea tray. He realized he was hungry, and looked with interest at what had been brought. Tea, of course, some broth, and some bread and butter. He sighed. He had hoped for something more. This invalid diet was monotonous, but he needed to get well.

He rubbed his hip with his good hand and then picked up his tea cup. It did not take him long to consume the meager fare and he was still hungry when the plate and cups were empty. A large chunk of tender venison sounded quite good.

****

The doctor came the next day and pronounced that the extensive bruising across his face was turning green—a sure sign of healing. His hip felt less painful, as did his shoulder which had managed to stay in joint. He went down to breakfast and managed to make it all the way back up the stairs to his room on his own.

Tired from being indoors, William called Larkin and dressed to go downstairs. His mother was nowhere to be seen, so he sat beside the fire and stared into it for a while. He imagined Sarah sitting across from him in her golden brown dress and looking at him with those eyes…

A movement glimpsed from the corner of his eye startled him. His mother was making her way across the parlor to the fire, wrapped in a large shawl.

"Are you cold, Mother?"

"It is a curse of age to never be able to get warm."

"Here, let me put more coal on the fire."

"You are good to me."

He snorted in laughter. "That's not what you usually say."

"I mean it, William. You are very patient and giving where I am concerned. I got a letter from my friend Constance—the Duchess of Evesbury—and she was telling me how her daughter-in-law insisted she move to the dower house even though half of it burnt down last year and it has not been repaired fully."

"That's nothing to do with us, surely."

"No, but I simply ask you to put me up while the

drains are fixed at Marwinne, and you do so with no hesitation."

"Well, Mother, I'm not likely to throw you out, despite what this duchess of whatever has done to her mother-in-law. The son should not have allowed it."

"Quite right, but men, you know, are often ruled by their...hearts, if you will."

Suddenly William felt uneasy. "I suppose so."

"I am simply grateful that you still value me, and my advice."

"Well, certainly, where we agree..."

"So when I tell you that Miss Mondragón is not for you, I know you will listen to me."

"Mother, this is dangerous ground."

"And yet I will speak. She is not for you, William. You must let her go. Look what happened when you went after her, and do not bother to deny it for I know that is what you were doing. She has gone back to her grandfather's, a mere earl, and they are no doubt introducing her to society that will accept her. Let her be settled amongst them. Find yourself a wife who will be accepted by your circle and who will be happy with it all."

Anger coursed through him, and he struggled to contain himself. All his life his mother had exerted influence over him, and he finally realized that it was time to free himself from her.

"Mother, we will not speak of this again. In this, and all matters related to me, you will please mind your own business."

He rose and stalked from the room.

Chapter Twenty-Four

The night of the supper dance arrived, delayed two nights to ensure Wendell's complete recovery. Sarah looked at herself in the mirror, admiring once again her twilight blue evening gown. The sight of it brought back memories of the disastrous ball, but she choked back the emotions and straightened. Her aunt had set all the dances, and only chosen those that Sarah felt competent with. Even so, it would be her first dance in company for most of them.

She went downstairs to the little ballroom where most of the guests had congregated. Supper would be held in the adjoining room, and the quartet was set up and playing a quiet melody that still allowed for talking.

Lavinia waved her over and she bit her lip before going to her side. She took Sarah's arm in hers and said over the music, "I am so glad to have been invited!"

"We still need to ride sometime."

"Your estate is larger than ours. I'll just have to bring Pickle over here."

"Pickle?"

"That's my horse's name—at least what I call her. My mother hates that I do so…and so I do it more often than not!"

Sarah giggled a little and Lavinia held her out a little. "I do so love this gown."

Sarah pretended to preen a little and Lavinia

laughed into her hand. Becoming serious, suddenly, Sarah said, "I was so embarrassed at that ball…"

"Oh my dear, it happens. It really isn't so devastating as I know it must have felt. The dance went on and most of the room did not know what happened."

"I'm sure it wasn't long before they did."

"It was talked of, but so was the fact that the band's tempo constantly shifted making dancing all that much harder. I hope this one is better. And the puddings were bland. Everyone thought so."

"Thank you for trying to make me feel better, but you will never convince me that it wasn't a spectacular failure."

"And yet, here you are. And look, a young man approaches."

Sarah looked up in time to see Peter.

"I say, will the first do for our dance?"

"Yes, since Grandfather expects me to open."

"Well, then, shall we?"

Sarah allowed herself to be led off as the band's opening bars played. She was happy to see Lavinia approached by another young man and then fiercely concentrated on the dance to come. They stepped off, and began. Sarah started to look down, but Peter caught her gaze and held it.

"Just look at me. We'll be fine."

So she kept her eyes on his face, and soon found that she could read his intended movements by subtle shifts in his arms and shoulders, where his eyes glanced. It was much like riding a horse and communicating with leg pressure and reins.

A freeing discovery.

Before she knew it, the music had stopped and she

stood beside Peter, chest heaving from the exertion, but smiling with renewed confidence.

"I say, thought you said you were awful. You're jolly good!"

"So are you, it turns out."

He shook his head, leading her back to the seats. "I completely fudged on the turns and things. I do just enough to get by and keep my mother happy. Not that she notices what I do. I wonder if Wendell found someone worthy enough to dance with."

Just then Wendell and a girl in an exquisite gown strolled by and he chortled.

"Got the only daughter of a duke I'll bet!"

Sarah peered at the girl, trying to remember her introduction. "No, but she is the daughter of a marquess."

"Ah well, good enough I guess. What shall we do now?"

"Well, unless you plan to dance with me again, I think you need to mingle with the other available girls."

He sighed, "Alas. My mother already lectured me about dancing with you. I had best go find someone else."

She smiled, "Yes, I know how your mother feels about me."

He stopped suddenly and looked at her. "Just so you know how I feel about you."

Her eyes flew wide, but he was gone, swallowed by the milling people and she was alone. Lavinia found her and took her arm.

"Oh well done, my dear! Beautifully danced!"

"Thank you, you as well!"

"Oh, well it was heavy going with my partner. A

tip, my dear, if the Honorable James Watson asks you to dance, plead a twisted ankle and say no."

Sarah smiled, but did not laugh. She was not so comfortable with her own dance skills to laugh at other's faults. Just then a young man came up to her and bowed.

"Will you do me the honor of dancing the next with me?"

"Of course, Mr.…."

"It's Honorable, actually. James Watson."

Sarah allowed herself to be led off, but twisted to wave to Lavinia who slowly shook her head.

The next dance was one that Sarah had practiced since the first time her dance master had instructed her. She felt confident with it, especially after the first few turns where she saw how it worked with lots of bodies in movement. Unfortunately, Lavinia was accurate in her assessment of Mr. Watson's dance skills, but at least he was willing, which many of the young men did not seem to be.

When the dance ended, Sarah went into the supper room and sat beside her Aunt Genevieve who was in discussion with a large woman seated next to her.

"And I told him that whatever he did, he was not to take the last piece of the cake as that was to be saved for Annabelle. We had a profitable outing, gathering far more berries than we could ever use, and came back to find that all the cake was now gone."

"Oh, so vexing," said Aunt Genevieve.

"Indeed. But he is such a dear boy that one cannot stay angry with him for long. I believe I saw your girl dancing with him but a moment ago."

"With whom were you dancing, Sarah?"

"The Honorable James Watson."

"Yes, indeed! That is my boy! And is he not a good dancer?"

"He is certainly a welcome one." Sarah said.

Just then another young man approached and Sarah struggled to remember his name...Lord Reginald Winslow. Yes, that was it. He bowed slightly.

"If you are not otherwise engaged, will you dance the next with me?"

"Oh, yes of course. Thank you."

She stood and rested her hand on the top of his as they headed for the dance floor. He was a thin young man, with an impressively thick head of hair. His lower jaw protruded but not unpleasantly so. As the dance began, she was surprised to see he was an excellent dancer.

"You are quite good at this!" she exclaimed.

"Thank you, I have worked at it."

"I am still rather new to this."

"So I had heard. You are from Withcombe, originally, are you not?"

"Yes, my father is there."

"The horsemaster."

"Yes."

"Then, I presume you are an excellent horsewoman."

"I certainly love to ride."

"I had heard you made an excellent showing at the hunt sponsored by your grandfather."

Sarah executed a rather complicated turn and said, "You seem to have heard quite a bit about me."

"Let's just say I've been interested."

Sarah glanced up at him and half smiled before

they were separated by a partner exchange. She was not sure she liked Lord Winslow's interest in her. Thankfully, there was little time for talking during the rest of the dance. He bowed very nicely at the end and released her.

Blowing out a little breath, she spun in place, and moved through the crowd until she came to a side hall. She slipped down the hall to the gallery where her mother's portrait hung. Moonlight filtered in through the windows, but she could not really make out any features in the gloom. But she knew what she would have seen if she could, her mother standing beside a tree with a dog reaching its nose up to her hand. A calm expression, and yet a playfulness to her eyes and mouth. Sarah could see the likeness between her mother and herself, and longed to talk with her, at least one more time.

"Sarah?"

She jumped and turned to see her grandfather there. "Grandfather, I'm sorry. I shall go back."

"No rush, no rush. I understand needing a respite from the crowd. Your aunt missed you, and someone said they saw you slip away, so I came in search to make sure you were all right."

"Yes, sir, I am well. As you said, I just needed a small break from the festivities."

"Then allow me to escort you back." He held out his arm and she smiled as she took it. "Ah, this takes me back. I courted your grandmother at a ball. We slipped away during one of the dances and I kissed her on the terrace. Most scandalous."

"You rarely talk about my grandmother. What was she like?"

"She was a paradox, but we will talk more later."

The music from the ball room swelled as they neared it. Lord Peter spied her from beside his mother and rushed forward, grinning.

"Ah! There you are! Come on, I feel like dancing."

The earl quickly transferred her to Lord Peter's arm and Sarah just barely caught the hint of distaste that colored the duchess's face. Lord Peter led her to the floor just as the other dancers were stepping off. They caught up, flubbing the first steps a little in their haste, but then fell into the rhythm and swung into it.

As they danced, she glanced around the room, taking in the different couples and noting the somewhat bored expressions on some of the faces. What would it be like to have grown up in this world? Would she find it boring as well? Or would she still find it to be a challenge to meet and overcome every day? She thought back to her time at the stables, and never remembered being bored. Too many things happened everyday and too much needed to be done.

The evening wound down with people eventually taking their leave in the early hours of the morning. Sarah covered a yawn with her hand and her great aunt sent her to bed. Elsie met her and helped her get undressed before rushing off to take part in the after-ball party down in the kitchen.

"I hope I'm in time to get a bit of cake!" she said as she bustled out with Sarah's dress.

Sarah lay in bed, her mind too full of things to fall easily into sleep. In her heart she had hoped that somehow, the duke would appear at the dance and whisk her off. She sighed and rolled over as though to escape the thought. What was she thinking? He was at

Withcombe…and probably not alone.

Her heart twisted at the thought.

****

She must have fallen asleep, for she awoke to light filtering into her room from around the edges of the curtains. She groaned at how sore her body felt from so much dancing. After sitting up, she pushed out of her bedclothes and pulled her dressing gown around her, wondering if breakfast were still available.

A glance at the clock showed her it was nearly one o'clock, and she rather doubted breakfast was still on. With a sigh, she rang the bell, hoping Elsie had gotten some cake and sleep.

By the time a tray was brought up and she was dressed, Sarah was feeling more awake and less sluggish.

"There was ever so much food left over; it were heavenly!" Elsie prattled as she finished arranging Sarah's hair. "I got a huge piece of cake and told the cook what a splendid job she done of it."

"I'm so glad you enjoyed it. I don't know that I got a taste of it. I was so busy with dancing and talking."

"Eh, I'm sorry, miss. There, that's done and you are free."

Sarah looked it over and nodded, happy with the result. "Thank you, Elsie. Can you bring me my *pelisse*? I think I'd like to walk over to the stables."

Sometime later, she stepped out the servants' entrance and walked across the back of the kitchen garden toward the stables. The sunlight was obscured with clouds, and tiny crystals of ice floated in the air. Sarah wondered if a storm might be coming.

The stables were warmer, but the horses' breath

still condensed before them. Sarah stopped at each one, patting the neck or nose if available. When she came to Arthur's stall, she found him writhing on the ground in his stall.

She called to the stable hands and snatched up the lead from the wall before securing it to his halter. She pulled to try to get him to stand, but he resisted and she called again to the lads to come and help her.

Soon, they had congregated and almost succeeded in getting him up, but he collapsed again, thrashing about in pain. The head groom arrived with a pistol and put Alsington's King Arthur out of his misery.

Sarah stood beside the horse, eyes dry. She had witnessed many such deaths, and none were easy. She looked up at the boys standing outside the stall. "I'll go tell my grandfather."

The walk back stretched on before her. She made her way inside, then went first to the earl's study where she found him in conference with the steward. He looked up and frowned.

"Yes, Sarah, what is it?"

"Arthur is dead. He must have twisted his gut and was just put down."

"Oh, my dear, I am so sorry. Are you very distressed?"

She shook her head. "No…but yes of course. He was a good horse and I am grateful to have been able to ride him. I'm just a bit stunned right now."

"Go take a walk, my dear. I find it helps me in such situations."

"Yes, Grandfather, I will."

She wandered back out into the hall. She paused for a moment, and then looked down to see that her *pelisse* had gotten dirty in the scuffle with Arthur. She stopped a passing servant and asked her to find Elsie, then climbed the stairs up to her room to wait.

Elsie popped in, took one look at her *pelisse* and frowned. "Miss, what have you been doing?"

"A horse was ill…and died. I'm afraid I got rather mussed in the affair."

"Oh miss, I am sorry. I know how you loves them horses."

"Yes, Elsie. Thank you. I think I will go to the library to write a letter."

"Yes, miss."

She suddenly wished she could have two things: to talk to her father, and to be in the duke's arms.

Chapter Twenty-Five

Dark clouds covered the land, blanketing it in a false sense of warmth, where there was only bitter cold. Snowflakes flitted about, not quite landing, but not stopping either. William looked out the window, and felt a sudden need to go to the stables.

He gestured to Jarvis. "My coat, please."

When it was brought he shouldered into it, ignoring the slight scratch of the wool against his neck. He buttoned it up hastily and stepped out the front door.

The swirling wind nearly took his breath away. Mostly healed from his injuries, he now boasted only vestiges of bruising. His nose, he noted, was a different shape and it gave him a more earthly air. He thought he approved, but wondered what Sarah would think.

He wished for the scarf he had left off and held the collar closed around his face for some protection. More snowflakes skittered around him as he went, and he questioned his decision.

The horses stood away from their doors and stable boys ran about, finishing chores up before the storm hit. Arnas opened the door to yell for one of them, and stopped when he saw William.

"Just wanted to come check on the horses."

"They should be well. We've closed up the stalls and brought the horses in from pasture." He looked at the duke. "You should be inside as well, your grace."

"I just wondered if you had heard yet from Sarah."

Arnas's mouth worked for a moment. "Yes, she writes that her horse has died—twisted bowel—and she has asked for a Withcombe Bay to replace it."

Without thinking, William said, "Bard. Send her Bard."

Arnas nodded. "I thought that as well. We shall have to wait for this storm to clear, however."

"Yes. All right, I will leave you to it. Get yourself inside."

He struggled through the flying snow and wind up the rise to the manor, glowing through the growing maelstrom.

Once back inside, he sat beside the fire in the parlor to warm up. It would be time, soon, to dress for supper and he relished the silence of the house around him. His mother had returned to Marwinne within the last couple of days—the drains being repaired to general satisfaction. He was relieved to be free of her continual disapproval.

Warmed now, he rose to go change. By the time he reached his room, Larkin had already laid out his evening clothes and waited to help him change. He thought about it, and shook his head.

"Never mind, Larkin. I am the only one dining tonight. There will be no one to see whether I am dressed or not. In fact, I might simply fill a plate in the kitchen."

Larkin's face went blank, his eyes large. "Sir, I don't know what the kitchen staff would make of that."

"Don't worry, I won't. Just nonsense talk."

But he had been half serious. Still he remembered something his father said about servants preferring to be left to do their job as they were trained to do. He did not want to unsettle anyone, but neither did he want to sit in a large dining room alone.

Loneliness washed over him as he made his way downstairs. He had no one to talk to as an equal, no one to argue with him when needed. He was surrounded by people who feared his station and his power. He had the ability to do great harm. Or great good.

What did that look like, actually? Somehow, he thought Sarah would know.

He missed her, in so many ways. As soon as the storm was over, he would deliver Bard to her and then see where things went. But first…the storm.

The sky darkened as the clouds thickened. The snow grew heavier, until at last there was nothing to be seen from looking out the windows, just a swirling expanse of snowflakes scouring the glass panes. Frost grew from the inside where moisture condensed and then instantly froze, the crystals growing in star-like patterns.

He pushed back from the glass and a maid scuttled forward to close the curtains. He moved to the chair beside the fire and leaned on it, staring into the flames. Damn the storm! He wanted to be off…

****

Next morning dawned in the silence that falls after a heavy snow. William threw back the covers and went to the window, shoving the curtain aside. There, blanketing the world, lay at least a foot of snow, too deep to set off in. He swore.

It took nearly three days for the roads to be passable. Meanwhile he stalked about Withcombe, anxious to be off. He did not understand this urgency, but it pushed him. Finally, the snow had melted enough to allow him to go in pursuit.

He ordered the carriage and had Bard tethered to it, then set off.

They made it as far as the main road when the wheel fell into a hole and stuck. William got out and waited as the groom and the driver struggled to get the carriage free. Finally he lent his shoulder to the job and they managed to roll it free, his ankles and feet getting sloshed in icy mud. William climbed inside with a sigh of relief and leaned back against the seat.

Three miles later they repeated the whole thing.

And again.

By the time they made it to a tiny hamlet with a single inn, they were all muddy, cold, and sore from the effort. They made it only half as far as they should have, and the driver estimated another five days before they reached West Redditch and Wrottlesby.

The delay ate at him. Every moment that passed was another without Sarah.

The roads improved by the time they reached the halfway point of Bromley. There was still daylight, and though the driver wanted to stop in the village, William insisted they push on to the next town in an effort to make up time lost.

The driver shook his head, but chirruped to the horses and they continued on.

Night fell, and the lamps were lit to light the road and keep them from straying off. Now and then the sound of a horse clopped past and William tensed with each one. He began to think they should have stopped in Bromley.

A low shout and the carriage stopped. William

edged close to the door and tensed. The door handle turned and the door burst open as a burly form pushed inside. William did not hesitate, he struck out with a fist that connected with the man's hand and a gun clattered to the floor.

The bandit scrambled after it and William kicked viciously out. His foot jarred with the man's jaw and he kicked again and again, until the figure lay still. Then he picked up the pistol.

Climbing over the prone form, he emerged, pistol at the ready. One man on horseback held another pistol at the driver, but he took one look at William and spurred his horse on down the road. William turned to the body in the carriage and pulled him free with help from the groom and they dragged him to the side of the road. William took his horse and tethered it beside Bard, then ordered the driver to take them back to Bromley.

Two hours later, they pulled up at the main inn on the edge of the town. Low, wooden beams crossed the ceiling and William had to duck here and there. The owner met them on the doorstep, yawning and pulling his jacket on.

"I need to report an attack."

"Wha' 'appened?"

William explained and the tavern owner squinted at him in the light of the single candle he held.

"You did wha'?"

"I fought him off. Left him unconscious by the side of the road. I have his horse. I thought I could leave it here. Didn't want him going off after someone else."

"Prolly that Dick Smead and 'is gang. Been terrorizin' these parts. You shouln' a been out after dark."

"Yes I know. Stupid of me. But here we are."

The man huffed a bit, but gave him a room and told him where to have the driver and groom lodge the horses. "Just leave Dick's horse tied up out front. Mayhap 'e'll wake up and come back for it. We'll get 'im then."

It was well past midnight before William climbed between the coarse linen sheet and rough woolen blanket of the bed. The rush of adrenaline had long since died, and he closed his eyes once, and did not open them again until morning.

He was stiff and sore when the sunlight filtered through the thin curtains. Moving slowly, he rose and dressed, then went downstairs for a breakfast of sausage, coffee, and toast. He thanked the taverner and climbed into the carriage in front of the inn.

He called up to Gordon, the driver, "You all right after our adventure?"

"Aye, your grace. We're fine. Ready to get done with this, though."

"I happen to agree. Let's to it."

The groom shut the door for him, but he noticed it was loose. His attacker had strained the mechanism the night before. One more thing to get repaired...

As they passed through the part of the road where they were attacked, William looked carefully at the side of the road to see if there were any sign of the downed highwayman. Though he could see the drag marks of the body, there was nothing there.

It made him uneasy to think that somewhere an outlaw might have a grudge against him. But for now, the sun was out periodically and the ground seemed to be dryer. They were making better time than before.

This time, when the shadows lengthened and the sky darkened, they stayed at the first town they came to. William spent some time seeing that Bard was well stabled and that his men were comfortable, then went to a late supper and an early bed.

They would reach Wrottlesby tomorrow.

Chapter Twenty-Six

Sarah awakened to the silence after a snowfall. The room was cold. Elsie had not yet stoked the fire. She swung her legs out from the bed to hop across the chilly floor to the window. One glance showed her that ice all but covered the glass.

She scuttled back to the bed and curled up once again underneath the covers. She was barely back before the door opened and Elsie came in, carrying a load of coal.

"Good morning, Elsie."

The coal hod slipped from the maid's grasp and nearly clattered to the floor but for her quick hands. "Eh, miss, you startled me! Good morning."

"I'm sorry, Elsie. Are you well?"

"Aye, well enough." She knelt at the fireplace and added, "Do you want me to bring you up a tray?"

"Not yet. I'll go down in a bit. I'm just sorry you have to brave the cold each morning."

"I don't mind it. At home I'd be up before now milking cows with Father. This way I get to sleep in."

Sarah smiled. There had been long nights with the horses when one was ill or during a hard birth. For now, she relished the ability to snuggle under warm covers and wait to emerge until the fire took the brunt of the cold off.

"I think I am riding with Miss Esterhay today."

"Even as cold as it is?"

"It will warm up as the day goes along."

"Better you than me. I'll be safe inside, cleaning your morning dress." She picked up the hod and carried it out, leaving Sarah alone.

It took some time for the fire to take the edge off the cold, and by that time sun shone through the icy windows, leaving rainbow patterns on the floor. She quickly pulled on her furred slippers and fastened her dressing gown around her. Then she picked up the blanket that Emma had given her all those months before and wrapped it around her shoulders.

Cold air eddied around her as she opened the door to the hall, grateful for the blanket. The dining room had just been set by the time she arrived, and she filled a plate with her favorites before sitting down where she could look out the window.

What was the duke doing and did he think of her the way she thought of him? Her eyes closed and that last kiss replayed itself in her mind, him reaching for her, his mouth coming down upon hers and…

She stood, a little shakily, and headed back upstairs to her room.

Elsie was in the process of pulling out a morning dress for her to wear. Sarah dreaded the thought of undressing in the frigid air, but thankfully the fire had done its job and it wasn't as cold as it had been.

Today was a new dress, white background with small blue and light brown flowers printed upon it. As Sarah looked in the mirror, she was utterly delighted with it. She had never thought she would grow to love clothes so much, and wondered if her mother had.

She wore her long sleeves, and Elsie helped her

into a blue spencer for warmth. Then came the process of combing out her hair and arranging it upon her head. Sarah let her mind drift with each stroke of the brush and ended up where she so often did, with the duke coming ever closer to kiss her…

"There. Not bad, if I does say so myself." Elsie patted the last strand into place and stepped back.

Sarah simply grinned and trotted down the stairs to the parlor. Sitting at the piano, she practiced her songs for a while, then picked up her newest piece and began to struggle through it. A slight noise startled her and she looked up.

The earl stood there in the entryway. She realized he had sniffled, and that was the sound that alerted her.

"Grandfather!"

"Shh. Don't let me disturb you. I enjoy hearing you play, is all."

"I hope I didn't disturb you."

He was, after all, standing in his dressing gown.

"Nonsense. It does my heart good to hear music in these lonely halls."

She rubbed a hand lightly across the ivory keys. "It is a beautiful instrument."

"And yet, it has been silent for many years." He nodded to her and headed off in the direction of the breakfast room.

She played for a while longer, slightly self-conscious. When she saw her grandfather return up the stairs, she paused and pushed back from the piano, wondering when Lavinia would arrive.

Hours later, when the sun was overhead, she heard the gravel in the drive crunching and looked out the window to see a carriage pull up to the front steps. Her aunt was just coming down the stairs and motioned her into the parlor. They sat waiting for their guests to be shown in.

Sarah stood immediately to ring for a horse to be brought for her. She had requested one of the old Withcombe Bays to be saddled for her and was anxious to ride. The horse was finally brought around and the two girls hurried to the front steps to be helped onto their horses.

Despite wanting to race across the field, Sarah was mindful of her companion and the age of her horse. They rode staidly along, following the track to the woods and then skirting the edge. Lavinia was quiet for a time, and Sarah was content to be so as well.

"How are you liking life here?"

Sarah let a few footfalls pass before saying, "I find myself happy for the most part. If I had my father and the stables here, I think I would be completely happy. Except for…" She paused.

"Yes?"

Sarah shook her head. "It is silly to think of."

"It, or *he*?"

Sighing, she said, "You are right. He. There is someone. What about you?"

Lavinia blew out a little breath. "Marshall, Lord Brixton for me. And yet my father's money is from trade and I have no gentlemen or women in my pedigree."

"Well, I have my father, who I am so proud of. But apparently society looks down upon him."

"So we are both disappointed in love."

"Yes."

"My mother assures me I will get over this and

grow attached to someone who will marry me. But her words! *Attached* after what I have felt for his lordship."

Sarah compared it to her feelings for the duke and nodded. "It is a poor word to describe my feelings."

"Yes. But, there it is. Lord Brixton will probably choose someone whose background is more in line with his expectations, and I will fall victim to the same. Sometimes I think it is a rotten world."

Sorrow fell upon Sarah as they rode. This, then, was common. She was not the only one to be so disappointed in love.

In an effort to dispel the gloom, Sarah said, "Come, let's race to that building."

Lavinia laughed and urged her horse on, but Sarah was right behind. Though she let the horse gallop, she made sure not to push him too hard and thus Lavinia won. They pulled up to the building and then turned around and walked back toward the house. Sarah pointed to the gardens and they guided the horses in that direction.

"Oh, you have such a lovely park here."

"It isn't mine. This is all my grandfather's."

"Well, you have the run of it. Ours is small and bordered by tall hedges so one can't see beyond. Quite claustrophobic."

They cantered gently around the front lawn, laughing as they sailed over the low fence erected for Sarah's practice. Finally, they ended at the front steps where grooms took control of their horses and led them off.

Lavinia happily unbuttoned her riding coat and handed it to the butler, as did Sarah. The parlor was warm, and Aunt Genevieve had a tea cart with small sandwiches and cakes for the girls to choose from.

"We watched you from here. You seemed to be having fun."

Sarah grinned and bit into a finger sandwich. "Yes, indeed. Such fun having someone to ride with!"

"I agree. Much more so than my little brother and his pony. He can't control him and simply whines most of the time."

"Really, Lavinia, he's a sensitive child," Mrs. Esterhay said.

Lavinia simply flashed her eyes at Sarah and bit into a crispy tart.

Hiding a smile, Sarah glanced outside. For all her joy, there was a piece missing. She wondered yet again what William was doing.

The Esterhays left, and Sarah watched their carriage until it disappeared around the bend. Once upstairs in her room, Elsie helped her change into an afternoon dress before she went downstairs again. The front bell rang and she glanced up when the butler approached.

"Miss Mondragón, there is a gentleman to see you. He did not wish to come in." Frowning, Sarah followed him to the front door.

There stood William, with Bard.

Time stood still as they stared at one another. As though in a dream, she moved forward to cup Bard's head in her hands. She stroked his nose, gaze still on William. Then, without thinking, she melded against him. He enfolded her in his arms and buried his head down on her hair.

"Sarah…"

"Oh, William."

"Marry me."

"Yes."

He kissed her then, his mouth moving upon hers with tenderness and hunger.

When they broke apart, breathless, she said, "You brought me Bard!"

"Yes. I thought he would help convince you to marry me!"

She reached out to stroke the golden brown nose and grinned. "I would have said yes anyway, but this does, indeed, help!"

He gave her a light shake. "You are a wicked girl." His expression softened then and he added, "And I love you."

"I love you, too."

"What is all this?" The earl's voice sounded behind them and they broke apart.

"William brought me Bard, and then asked to marry me, so I said yes."

"William, is it?"

"Yes, sir. I am going to marry him. But I'd like your blessing."

"What does your father say to all this?"

Sarah bit her lip. "I don't know. I shall have to write to him to see what he says. I don't think he will be entirely happy."

The earl kissed her on the forehead. "Well, my dear. I give you my blessing, at least." He looked at William and added, "Well, well. The groom can take the horse and you both can come in."

"Oh, sir, may I take him to the stables?"

"Not in that dress!" Aunt Genevieve said from the doorway. "You can check on him later."

Sarah watched Bard be led around the side of the manor before allowing herself to be drawn into the house itself. William managed to sit beside her on the settee, the warmth and hardness of his thigh next to hers. After a minute she rose, almost overwhelmed with emotion.

"Please excuse me, I must go write to my father."

"Of course. Send him my regards." William's gaze never left hers.

"Thank you." She ducked her head and all but ran from the room down the great hall to the library. Then, pen shaking, she wrote:

My dear Aitatxo,

The duke has come, and I am to marry him. Please understand and be happy for us. As I have had to tell my grandfather, I am not my mother.

Thank you for sending me Bard. I love you.

Sarah

Her heart was too full to write more. She sealed it and set it by the front door with the other letters to go out. When she returned, it was to find her grandfather very graciously inviting William to stay at Wrottlesby.

"You will be far more comfortable here than at the Dog and Lion."

With a glance at Sarah, he accepted. "I must go get my case. I'm afraid I did not bring an evening suit."

The earl waved it away. "That is of no consequence. Perhaps we shall all eat in afternoon attire this evening."

Genevieve looked pointedly at him. "I shall hold you to that."

William returned from seeing his things settled in his room and Sarah stood, saying, "I promise to be careful, Aunt, but I must see that Bard is well settled."

"Just be careful, my dear."

"Yes, ma'am."

"I'll accompany you," William said.

She led him through the halls and down the back stairs through the servants' entrance. They crossed the green and made their way to the low buildings, Sarah holding onto his arm, stealing glances at him from time to time. They entered through the large double doors and Sarah called a groom over.

"Where is the new horse, Bard?"

The boy trotted off and they followed him to a large box stall where Bard currently paced around. He nickered when they called to him and came to the door. Sarah hugged his neck and he rubbed against her shoulder with his head. William scratched behind his ears before patting him gently.

"Do you like them now?"

William looked at her, then back at Bard. "I do. After Tunbridge Oak, I swore I'd never set foot in a stable. But you...you and Bard have brought me back. I don't know that I could ever love them as you do, but I certainly respect them."

"*Aitatxo* taxed me with helping you like them again. He will be happy to know I succeeded." She lifted her face to his and he bent to kiss her, ignoring the stable hands scurrying past with armloads of hay.

She pulled away, smiling. "We shouldn't... Not here."

He sighed and offered her his arm. Together they headed back to the house.

Chapter Twenty-Seven

It took nearly a week for William to return to Withcombe. Sarah had asked for a Christmas wedding, and he went to make the estate ready for its new mistress. Sarah stood on the doorstep as he paused and returned for one more kiss, growling with frustration when it was over.

Sarah watched the mail, waiting for a response from her father, long before it was possible for it to arrive. It came finally, one week after William left.

My dearest daughter,

I can hear your happiness, and for that I rejoice. I waited to write you, not knowing what to say, then waited not knowing how to say it. His grace, for such he will always be to me, assures me of his love and constancy. I know you too well, and know that you will fight for your happiness. Unlike your mother, who sank beneath the waves of sorrow for what she lost, I think you will be open to whatever life brings you. I am so proud of you, Potxola, and very happy for you too.

Your loving Aitatxo

Sarah grinned broadly at this and skipped off, only to be called by her aunt.

"Sarah, come give me some ideas about your trousseau."

"What?" She stared wide-eyed at her aunt.

"Your clothes, wedding clothes."

"Oh. Of course. Yes." She forced herself to sit and look through samples of cloth and trimmings, though her mind still whirled, the words of her father's letter revolving about her brain.

Finally, a week before Christmas, the three of them, accompanied by Elsie on the top of the carriage, headed for Withcombe.

Sarah strained to look out the window as they neared Wexley where they had to slow down to navigate through the town. Her grandfather and aunt were tired from the journey, and all were ready for the trip to be over. As they came to the end of the town, the church standing to the left side of the road, her heartbeat suddenly increased.

There, in two days' time, she would be married.

The duke was there to greet them as they stepped down from the carriage. Her grandfather and aunt would stay with him until the wedding, but she would return to her father's house to await the nuptials. The duke cupped her face in his hand, and then the carriage continued on down to the stables.

Sarah sought her father in the cottage. He lay asleep in the little parlor and she kissed his cheek, startling him awake. He jumped up to embrace her.

"It is you! Emma, she is here!"

Emma shuffled forward from the stairs and hugged her after Arnas released her. She noticed the two of them exchanging looks and frowned.

"What? What is it?"

Arnas reached out and Emma took his hand. It took Sarah a moment to comprehend and then she squealed with true delight and hugged them both.

"When did this happen?"

"We went before the vicar last week," Emma said. "Are you sure you don't mind?"

"Nothing could make me happier! Now I know you won't be alone!"

Sarah and her father were expected that evening for supper, but Arnas begged off. "I don't belong there. Maybe one day, but for now, leave me here with Emma."

So she walked to the manor house alone.

****

On the morning of the second day, she rose and dressed in her cream satin gown with her matching bonnet. Elsie helped her and they were ready long before her grandfather's carriage arrived to take her to the church. Her eyes followed the mossy stone up to the very top of the bell tower. Her grandfather met her at the door to the church, ready to walk her up to William. It was Arnas' own suggestion, and Sarah turned for one last look at her father and Emma taking their seats as her grandfather led her down the aisle.

William had taken out a common license, sparing them the reading of the banns. Instead, the bishop read from the Book of Common Prayer and they repeated their vows. She knew that William put a ring on her finger, and that they were presented to the congregation, and then she was led to William's carriage to return to Withcombe for the wedding breakfast.

William had spared no expense. Garlands of evergreen hung from the walls and over the mantle. Wax candles lit the interior, as did the fire crackling in the large fireplace. Ham and bacon, warm rolls and butter, and more filled the tables. Some beautiful jellies also graced the sideboard, as did hothouse grapes. Sarah was somewhat overwhelmed as she looked upon the seemingly endless fare. She was glad to see that her father and Emma attended, though they sat toward the end of another table.

Sometime later, when all the guests had finally departed, William led her to the duke's bedchamber. She looked around at the fresh bed curtains and counterpane in blue and white and yellow. William turned her attention to the painting hanging over the fireplace. She beheld the horse depicted there and read the name—Withcombe Bard.

With a squeal of delight, she vaulted into William's arms and he swung her around, laughing.

"Only you would find a painting of a horse to be an acceptable wedding present!"

She smiled up at him. "Only you would know that!"

They stared at one another and he bent to kiss her tenderly, then with more fervor.

"I think you will always be my little horsemistress."

"That's duchess to you."

A word about the author…

Born and raised in the west in California and Nevada, Grace Colline now lives in the deep south. As an adult, she travelled extensively in the US and Australia where she lived for several years. In all that time, she met lots of people from all walks of life.

She tries to include variety in her characters as well, and enjoys the opportunity to travel vicariously through them.

For now, she lives with her husband, two of her five children and several dogs. She teaches online biology as an adjunct professor in her spare time. In addition, she is an avid fiber artist who spins wool and other materials into yarn, and then knits it up into all manner of things.

****

https://gracecollinehistorical.com

****

If you enjoyed this story, leaving a review at your favorite book retailer or reader website would be much appreciated. Thank you!